THREE JAYS GO TO ROME

© PAT SMYTHE 1960

Three Jays Go To Rome was first published in the U.K. by Cassell & Co. Ltd, London, W.C.I, in 1960. This edition was published by May Fair Books Ltd, 14 St. James's Place, London, S.W.I, in 1968, and was printed in Great Britain by Love & Malcomson Ltd, Brighton Road, Redhill, Surrey, England.

Three Jays go to Rome

by
PAT SMYTHE

ILLUSTRATED BY
KEITH MONEY

ARMADA
PAPERBACKS
for Boys & Girls

CONTENTS

AUTHOR'S NOTE

In this year of all years, everyone knows that the Olympic Games exist. So do the various characters connected with the Games whom I have mentioned in this latest *Three Jays* book. Once again, however, I ought to mention for the benefit of new readers that the adventures described, the Jays themselves and their friend 'Dashitall' Darcy, are straight out of my imagination. Often, I wish they weren't!

To my good friend and dedicated agent, George Greenfield, I would like to dedicate this sixth book in the series.

Miserden　　　　　　　　　　　　　　PAT SMYTHE

CHAPTER ONE

A LITTLE LEARNING

IF I happen to be at home when term ends, I always drive over to Cheltenham and bring Jane and Jacky back to Miserden for the holidays. Last Christmas I was delayed in London, doing some last-minute shopping for presents, and only managed to get home just before midnight on the day that they broke up. I had telephoned Paddy, my secretary, to tell her that I would be held up and had asked her to fetch them from school. Jimmy, Jane's brother, had broken up a couple of days earlier and had made his own way back to Miserden, exulting, no doubt, in the fact that he had stolen a march over the girls. For the benefit of new readers of this series, I ought to explain that the Three Jays, so called because of their initials and also for the raucous din that always seems to come when they are together, were in fact the best of friends although they never missed an opportunity to score over each other.

On that particular night, the house was in darkness, except for a light downstairs that Paddy had left for me, when I drove down the lane and swung the car through the gates into the yard. I got out, stretched myself after the long drive from London and gratefully savoured deep breaths of our clean Gloucestershire air. It was a crisp night, with the stars scattered like diamonds on an expanse of black velvet. Somewhere out on the 'banks', as we call the rolling hills in the Cotswolds, a fox barked twice and I thought of the meet at Miserden, hoping the weather would hold till then. London is a fine city with its lights and Christmas decorations and all the bustle and excitement, but give me Gloucestershire with its slower and dependable country rhythms for lasting happiness. Laughing at myself for getting sentimental, I took another deep breath of the cold, clean air and then climbed up the steps leading from the yard into the house.

Paddy must have heard the car go by for she had come down to the kitchen and was making a hot drink for me. 'All in order?' I asked, raising an eyebrow towards the floor upstairs.

Paddy got my meaning at once. When the Jays hit Miserden like a cyclone, anything may happen—and it usually does! She paused in her bustling about and turned to grin at me, holding a cup and saucer in each capable hand. 'Yes,' she said, 'they're fast asleep, thank goodness. They wanted to stay up for you, of course, but I managed to talk them out of it.'

'Well done,' I said. 'I love the Jays dearly but it's been an exhausting day and their hearty greetings on top of everything would be just a shade much. Do they look well?'

'Grand,' she answered. 'Jacky's grown quite a bit. Her school uniform will have to be let down before she goes back—otherwise it'll be almost indecent!'

'Next thing we know she'll have grown too big for Pickles and then her father'll have to buy her a new pony,' I said. 'Thank Heavens he can afford it, easily enough.' I ought to mention, again for the benefit of any new readers, that although Jane and Jimmy were distant relatives of mine, Jacky's presence at Miserden was something of an accident—or, as Jimmy would have put it, 'a bloomin' disaster'. Her father was a widower, a very wealthy business man, whom I had met at some social gathering several years before. When he had told me about his only daughter, who was obviously the apple of his eye, and

8

had said that she was wild about riding, I had casually suggested that she ought to spend a short holiday at Miserden with us. He took me at my word and shortly afterwards there arrived at Miserden the most precocious little horror of a girl I had ever had the misfortune to meet— Miss Jacqueline de Vere Field, to give her full name. Readers of *Jacqueline Rides for A Fall* may remember just how spoilt she then was and how badly she behaved. Anyway, to cut a long story short, Jimmy and Jane, who were about the same age, had had a tonic effect on her and it wasn't long before she had learned to throw off her spoiled ways and reveal her true worth. Jacky would always be the impulsive kind, rushing into scrapes because she never paused to think first, but she had many good qualities and kept her end up in their trio.

I was thinking about all the many adventures they had had since those early days when Paddy broke into my reverie. 'Do drink your nightcap before it gets cold,' she urged. 'By the way, I forgot to mention—Miss Spencer would like you to get in touch with her. She's got something on her mind about the girls, I think.'

Miss Spencer was headmistress of Jane's and Jacky's school in Cheltenham. 'Oh dear, bad reports again, I suppose,' I groaned.

'No, their reports came in the post today and I thought you'd want me to open them. They're not at all bad— surprisingly good, in fact.'

'Perhaps the Jays are sickening for something,' I said suspiciously. 'Jane's usually quite a worker but don't tell me that Jacky's getting conscientious in her old age. I couldn't stand it!'

'Well, anyway, Miss Spencer would like a word with you. Will you speak to her on the phone tomorrow morning?'

'I tell you what, Paddy. There are one or two Christmas things I ought to buy in Cheltenham. Would you like to ring her secretary first thing, say I'll be in Cheltenham anyway and could I call on her in the morning? If there's anything wrong—which I hope not—she'd prefer to tell me in person, I'm sure. Oh, I do hope everything's all right—but you never can tell with the Jays! '

After which deep philosophical thought, I thanked Paddy for the hot drink, wished her goodnight and went upstairs to bed. A few minutes later, I heard her footsteps go past my door and the landing light went out. For a few short hours peace would reign over Miserden House—until daylight brought the Jays into their full stride.

*   *   *

In fact, they hardly waited for daylight. I was in that delicious half-way state between sleeping and waking quite early next morning when a commotion started outside my bedroom door. Two shrill soprano voices, joined by an uncertain treble which occasionally plunged into bass depths, began to sing:

'Good King Wenceslas looked out
On the Feast of Stephen.'

I sang back at them:

'Now you've chased my sleep right out,
Which was deep and crisp and even.'

It wasn't a very bright retort but at seven o'clock in the morning my brain was not functioning all that swiftly. There was a bang on the door and then the Jays in dressing-gowns and pyjamas rushed in. Jacky and Jane swooped at the bed to give me a hug; Jimmy hung back, a shade uncertain of what the reception might be. He need not have worried. It was impossible to be upset with the Jays for long.

In their usual way they all started to talk at once but after a few moments I managed to restore some semblance of order. I had switched on the bedside lamp as soon as they entered, for it was still pitch-dark outside, and I watched their laughing faces as they clustered round my bed.

'Oh, Pat, isn't it wonderful?' said Jacky. 'Four weeks holiday, Christmas in a few days, presents—everything! Are we going hunting on Boxing Day?'

'I do hope it won't be too slippery,' Jane said anxiously. 'I'm worried about Jacky.'

'Why?' I asked incautiously.

'Well, she can't stay on very well at the best of times,' Jane replied. 'If it's slippery, she might fall off and break her neck.'

'Well?' was Jimmy's contribution.

Jacky took a wild swing at them both but from years of practice they hardly troubled to duck.

'If you're not careful, none of you will go hunting,' I said. 'I hear Miss Spencer wants to see me about you two girls. What's the trouble this time?'

Jane and Jacky looked as demure as only two mischievous youngsters know how to. 'Trouble?' Jacky echoed. 'I don't know of any trouble, do you?' she turned to Jane, who added, 'Not us, Pat. If there's any trouble, it must be two other people.'

'I doubt it,' I said. 'You and trouble go together like fire and smoke. Come on, tell me what it is. There must be something up if Miss Spencer wants to see me.'

Jane looked thoughtful. 'We're not in any trouble—honestly, Pat. Our reports this term were pretty good—you just read 'em. And we didn't get any more order marks than usual.'

'That means quite a few, I bet,' Jimmy observed.

'Perhaps the old Spencer's worried that we're working too hard,' Jacky said smiling. 'She gave me quite a motherly pat when I went to say good-bye yesterday and told me not to overdo things. She probably meant holiday work.'

11

'More likely eating too much turkey,' Jimmy cut in. 'She knows even *your* stomach can't stand up to indefinite punishment!'

I glanced from Jane to Jacky and then back again. They looked innocent enough but somehow I sensed that something was up. There seemed to be a private joke between them, an indefinable air of conspiracy which for the moment excluded Jimmy. It had something to do with my forthcoming visit to Miss Spencer, I guessed, but I could not penetrate beyond that point. Except that Jane and Jacky were hardly in trouble: they appeared too sure of themselves, almost smug in fact. Ah well, it was no use trying to crystal-gaze. They were obviously not going to enlighten me and I would know soon enough what it was when I went to see Miss Spencer in a few hours' time.

'Well, now you've done your good deed for the day and ruined my beauty-sleep . . .' I began.

'You don't need any, Pat . . .' Jimmy broke in.

'Flatterer!' yelled the two girls in chorus.

'. . . As I was about to say when I was so rudely interrupted,' I went on firmly, 'you'd better go and get washed and dressed—and annoy Paddy for a change. If the frost hasn't hardened the ground too much, Paul will be taking the horses up to the paddock for exercise after breakfast. You finish your unpacking first and then you can join her with the ponies. They need plenty of work to get them fit but make sure you don't overdo it to start with. If one of them goes lame, then bang goes your hunting these holidays. Okay?'

Jimmy stood up from his perch at the foot of my bed and gave a mock salute. 'Permission to fall out, sir, please?' he said.

'Carry on, sergeant,' I answered.

'Will you be coming up to the paddock later, Pat?' Jane asked.

'I'll try—but I doubt it. Paddy and I've got heaps of

12

letters to deal with first and the roads are a bit skiddy between here and Cheltenham. Besides, I don't know how long Miss Spencer will keep me. If I can get back in time, I will but don't wait for me. Now, on your way, you Jays, and don't make too much clatter. Paddy may not be awake yet.'

'Oh, she is, Pat,' Jacky said. 'We made sure of that before we called on you!'

I picked up a book from the bedside table and threatened to throw it at them. With a shrill whoop they fled from my room.

After breakfast Paddy rang the school and fixed my appointment for ten-thirty. She and I went through the letters that had accumulated in the three days I had spent in London and around ten o'clock I went to the yard to get the car. Paul, my head groom, had already fetched up the horses from the lower stables and the Jays were busy saddling their ponies. I was reminded of Paddy's remark of how Jacky had grown during the term. Pickles, her breedy little chestnut pony, had carried her sturdily and well for the past few years but now she seemed a shade too big for him. I noticed that her jeans hardly covered her ankles and they had been collecting mud from the ground the previous summer holidays. I had always thought of life with the Jays as being untouched by time, something one came back to at intervals and started again from the very point where school or one of my show jumping trips abroad had forced us to leave off. But now I realized that time had not left us alone. The relationship might need adjusting as the Jays grew on through their teens. Still, there would be plenty of time to think of that later on. None of us was exactly ready to draw an old age pension just yet!

There had been a slight ground frost overnight but a bright wintry sun was thawing it out as I drove along the high ridge to Birdlip and then down the steep hill towards

13

Cheltenham. The road was still white with frost in places where the hedges or woods cast shadows across it and I drove more slowly than usual. It wouldn't do to skid into a ditch and have the car immobilized over Christmas. I just had time to do some shopping before turning into the long drive that led up to the school. It had been a large private mansion in former years but a new wing had been added and in the grounds near the main building there was now a laboratory block, all glass and steel in the modern style, and a gymnasium on the other side of the drive to balance it.

There is always something lonely, I find, about an empty school. I had worked hard during my own school-days, although even then my thoughts were fairly occupied with ponies and problems of jumping, although the square roots and irregular verbs had their share of thought! Perhaps the lapse of time since my last contact with school made me a shade uncertain as I rang the highly polished brass bell by the front door just as a nearby church clock chimed the half-hour. I admired Miss Spencer whom I was about to see, with her brisk air of no-nonsense and her sense of fair play, but somehow when I met her I usually felt rather like a junior girl on the mat for some school offence!

A trim maid answered my ring and ushered me down a corridor to Miss Spencer's room. As she knocked and then pushed the door open for me to enter, I could not help thinking of the last time I had been in this very room —when Jane and Jacky had been accused of cheating in an exam and only Jimmy's smart detective work had proved them innocent.* Miss Spencer rose briskly from her desk and came round to shake hands. We chatted for a few moments and then I remarked, 'You know, there always seems to be a crisis in the air whenever I come to see you. I hope there's nothing wrong this time.'

* See *Three Jays Go to Town*.

She smiled. 'There's no cause for alarm, Miss Smythe. Jane and Jacqueline are not in any scrapes, at least as far as I am aware! Indeed, it is really for quite the opposite reason that I asked you to call today.'

I must have shown my surprise for she continued with, 'Perhaps I should explain that last cryptic remark.' She pulled off her horn-rimmed reading glasses and ran a hand over her crisp, greying hair that was cut short in an Eton crop, as she settled back in her chair. A faint smile tugged at the corners of her mouth and I wondered again what could be up. Miss Spencer was certainly enjoying some private joke and I waited for her to enlighten me. Headmistresses occasionally like to hold the floor—they are usually too senior to be interrupted lightly—so I also settled back in my chair and controlled my impatience to hear her news.

She made a tent of her fingers and thumbs and gazed at me over the top. 'Would it surprise you, Miss Smythe, to know that Jane and Jacqueline have suddenly shown a keen interest in classical literature?'

'It wouldn't just surprise me—it would amaze me!'

'And that they recently asked the School Librarian to order a special list of books on the classics, including an expensive dictionary of mythology that has just been published?'

'I'm lost for words,' I said. 'Please go on.'

'And—what's more—they both asked if they could have extra tuition during their play-hour in Latin and Italian? And, when they had to write an end of term essay on "My Favourite Author", Jane chose Virgil and Jacqueline chose Horace? Incidentally, they each wrote quite a sound essay, full of facts that they must have read up somewhere.'

'I just don't understand it,' I said, shaking my head in wonder. 'We are talking about Jane and Jacky, aren't we?'

'Yes, indeed,' she replied. 'But wait till you hear the *pièce de résistance*. Two days ago—that is, the day before term ended—they asked their form mistress if they could have an interview with me. Naturally, it was granted and I saw them both after supper that night. They said that it seemed wrong to them to learn classics without having first-hand experience of how the ancient people lived and knowing just what their buildings and monuments looked like. I agreed that this was an admirable principle. Then Jacqueline asked me point-blank if I couldn't organize a party from their form to travel to Rome in the summer holidays and spend a week or two sight-seeing there. I could hardly believe my ears. Somehow I just couldn't imagine Jacqueline—or Jane either, for that matter— trudging along the Via Appia Antica with a guidebook in hand or studying the monuments in the Forum! But I was so taken aback that I agreed to look into it. That's why, first of all, I wanted a chat with you, Miss Smythe. Tell me—have I misjudged your wards all this time? I took them to be nice, normal healthy youngsters who weren't over-burdened with a sense of devotion to learning but perhaps I've been unfair. What do you think?'

The word Rome had given me a clue. Smiling in spite of myself at the perplexed look on Miss spencer's face, I said, 'Can I ask you a question first? Did they mention any special dates for going to Rome?'

'Funny you should ask that,' she commented. 'Yes, they did. Jane explained that it would be best to be there in the first fortnight in September so that they would be in the right mood for returning to school a few days after they got back. She also thought the weather might not be so distractingly hot there as it would be in August.'

'I bet she did,' I said and couldn't help laughing aloud. Miss Spencer looked more surprised than ever.

'What's the matter, Miss Smythe?' she asked, with a sharp note creeping into her voice. 'None of us likes to think that we are on the outside of a private joke.'

'I'm sorry,' I replied. 'Please don't think me rude, but

I'm almost sure I know the answer. There's no need to worry whether Jane and Jacky are suffering from brain-fever or a rush of Latin to the head. The solution is far more typical. You see, the Olympic Games are to be held in Rome next September and the equestrian show jumping events take place on the seventh and the eleventh. The B.S.J.A. announced the short list for the team training a week or two ago and my name happens to be amongst them. Doesn't Jane's and Jacky's enthusiasm for the classics date from about then?'

Now it was Miss Spencer's turn to laugh and before long I had to join in. 'Aren't they young scamps?' she said at last. 'They acted the part so well, too. Their form mistress and I were quite taken in by their sudden zeal. And all the time they just wanted to get to Rome to watch you jump in the Olympics.'

'Not so fast, please,' I interjected. 'I've only been selected for the training programme at present. It doesn't follow that I shall be chosen for the team itself. The horses matter too and they must be a hundred per cent fit at the time the entries close. After all, no horse, no jockey!'

'Anyway, they must think it's all right,' she said. 'And so do I!' she added stoutly. 'Ah well, it was a good attempt on their part. I hope they won't be too disappointed when they know we've tumbled to their stratagem.'

A vague plan was beginning to form in my mind. 'Do they have to be disappointed?' I asked.

'You mean—can't they go to Rome? Oh, I think it's out of the question, Miss Smythe. Think of the expense for one thing—and who would look after them for another? If you are in the British team, you'll be far too busy to look after them yourself. Besides, I couldn't spend school money on what would really be a private jaunt. The Governors would never stand for it!'

'There might be a way round,' I said, thinking aloud. 'First, do any of the mistresses drive?'

'Yes, several of them own cars and—touch wood—they never seem to be involved in accidents, so I assume they drive quite well. Why do you ask?'

'It was just a thought I had. A friend of mine owns a Dormobile—one of those miniature buses that has sleeping accommodation on board. She rarely uses it and I'm sure it could be borrowed or hired for a couple of weeks or so. I believe it takes six people in comfort. Now just supposing Jacky and Jane and a couple of friends from their form were to go along, plus two of the school-mistresses to share the driving and look after them. It would take about four days to get to Rome, a week there and four days on the return journey. They could all sleep on board, so the only real expense would be petrol and food, plus the cross-Channel fares. It wouldn't cost more than about thirty pounds a head. And think what a wonderful opportunity it would be for two of your staff to refresh themselves by looking at Rome?'

'Miss Smythe, you're as bad as Jane and Jacqueline at thinking out far-fetched schemes.' Something about her tone of voice belied the sharpness of her words and I decided to plunge on.

'It's not all that far-fetched,' I said. 'Lots of forward-thinking schools send their pupils abroad in the holidays. After all, we're part of the European community and we've been insular for far too long. Besides, it wouldn't hurt Jane and Jacky to turn the tables on them. They've pretended to be keen on culture—well, why don't we take them at their word, You could work out a route across France that would take in all the famous places, Versailles, Fontainebleau, Chartres, the Loire châteaux, Avignon—the lot, as they'd say. Make them really do it the hard way and study the ancient architecture and the places of interest. Better still, why not make them write an essay on some classical subject during these holidays. Set one for the whole form and announce that the four best will qualify

18

for a trip to Rome. If some of the girls' parents couldn't afford the extra expense of the trip, I'll put up a prize.'

'It might work,' she said doubtfully.

'I'm sure it would. They wouldn't even need to put up at an hotel in Rome while they were there—not that there will be any hotel accommodation going spare in Olympic year. There are several camping places on the coast about thirty miles west of Rome and it takes next to no time to get into Rome along the new *autostrada*.'

'We'd have to make the essay competition voluntary,' she said. 'Some of the girls' parents might want to make other holiday plans for them for the first half of September.'

'All the better for Jane and Jacky. They'd stand more chance of winning it then.'

'But what if one of them, Jane, say, happened to write one of the four best essays and qualified for the trip—and Jacqueline didn't? If I'm going to mark the essays, I should naturally show no favouritism.'

'Of course not,' I said. 'Surely it's up to them? They're the ones to show this supposed interest in the classics. If their bluff is called, they've just got to prove themselves.'

'Well, as long as they clearly understand that. You know, Miss Smythe, I really think there may be something in this idea of yours. First, I shall have to consult Miss Haywood, their form mistress. You remember her, don't you?'

'Indeed I do!' Miss Haywood had been involved a few terms before when it seemed that either Jane or Jacky had been guilty of cheating in an examination. Her evidence had made things look black for them at first but later she realized she had made a mistake and had had the good grace to admit it right away.*

Miss Spencer went on, 'Luckily, she's one of my staff who can drive and she's quite an adventurous type of

* See *Three Jays Go to Town*.

19

person. I think she might well agree to the plan. It's a pity this idea didn't come up a few days ago—before we broke up for the holidays. Now it means that, if the scheme goes ahead, letters will have to be written to the parents of every girl in the form and, with Christmas only a couple of days away, my secretarial staff have gone home and aren't due back till the end of next week.'

'We might be able to help out. My secretary, Paddy Bury, is an expert typist and she knows how to work a duplicating machine. Once Christmas is over, I know she'd be only too happy to pop into Cheltenham and do any typing you require.'

We spent perhaps another twenty minutes talking things over and the more we discussed it, the more enthusiastic Miss Spencer became about the project. I suspected that, for two pins, she would have liked to go along herself but she probably realized that the presence of the headmistress might throw a shadow over the holiday spirit. It struck me then how terribly lonely a position of great responsibility can be. I wondered what sort of Christmas she would have, alone in the empty, echoing school. Impulsively, I invited her to dinner at Miserden for the evening of Boxing Day and she seemed genuinely pleased to accept.

The Jays had not guessed the reason for my visit to the school, so Miss Spencer and I agreed to keep them in the dark until the letter announcing the competition arrived. Finally, I took my leave, saying that we could discuss everything in more detail on Boxing Day night, after the Jays had gone to bed.

*   *   *

On my return to Miserden, they naturally asked me what had happened but I managed to fob them off with the excuse that Miss Spencer wanted me to give a talk

20

about show jumping to some of the senior girls during the Easter term. (We had in fact mentioned this topic during the interview and had fixed a provisional date.) They seemed to be satisfied with this explanation, though the quick-witted Jane wondered aloud why it couldn't have been dealt with on the telephone.

Christmas was a thoroughly family affair. The Jays stayed up on Christmas Eve to come to midnight Mass in Miserden Church and it seemed that no sooner had they gone to bed than they were up again exploring their Christmas stockings with whoops and shrieks of excitement. We went to Matins and sang all the Christmas hymns and when we came back to the house and opened the front door, we were met by a lovely waft of 'parfum ding dong' as the Jays called the scent of turkey.

During the afternoon I dressed up as what had to pass as Father Christmas wearing an Argentine Poncho (a red blanket with a slit in the middle to put one's head through), black and red cowboy boots, a Huaso's belt (the Chilean cowboy) and a Red Indian Chief's head-dress with feathers down the back. I was given a great ovation dressed in this attire as I arrived downstairs and without wasting a moment I started dealing out the presents from under the Christmas tree. Even Fina la Ina, my little Lucas terrier, was waiting expectantly for her presents, because the dogs and cats always had some parcels for them and they all sat around the tree in the hall joining in the fun and getting covered in wrappings and sticky labels. Eventually the day was over after too much eating, playing energetic games, clearing up and finally dropping into bed exhausted.

On Boxing Day we were up at dawn for a day's wonderful hunting where Jacky distinguished herself by taking so short a cut across country that she ended up ahead of the fox! Luckily, there were so many foot followers and motorists spread over the country that her escapade went unnoticed by the Master.

That evening Miss Spencer came over to dinner and shook the Jays by being more human than they had ever imagined. We played charades and she not only thought up the most ingenious words to act but showed that the stage had lost a real actress when she decided to take up teaching. If the rest of the school could have seen her appearance on all fours as the reluctant cat in the last syllable of 'Olympus' (O-limb-puss) while Jimmy, her partner, tried to coax her, they would have had a fit of hysterics.

It took us a couple of days to get over Christmas, during which time Paddy discreetly nipped into Cheltenham when the Jays weren't looking. Then, on the Wednesday of the following week, two things arrived at Miserden—or, to be accurate, one thing and one person. The latter was our old friend, 'Dashitall' Darcy. The former was an official-looking letter with the school crest on the flap of the envelope.

CHAPTER TWO

. . . IS A DANGEROUS THING

IN case anyone has forgotten, I should explain that Flight Lieutenant Darcy de Vere is a cousin of Jacky's who keeps popping in and out of these stories. He has three great passions in life—flying high-speed aircraft, driving a vintage Bentley nicknamed 'Bertha' and drinking large quantities of beer. He unfortunately also has one pet hate—horses! Jacky's theory was that he had been bitten by one as a baby: Jane thought it more likely that Darcy had done the biting. Whatever the reasons behind it may be, there is no getting away from Darcy's dislike of those 'four-legged menaces' as he calls them and it says much for his affection for the Jays that he should of his own free will enter the horsy atmosphere of Miserden from time to time. Darcy is tall and lanky with a carroty thatch of hair and an enormous handle-bar moustache of a ginger hue. The Jays know him as 'Dashitall' because of his fondness for peppering his conversation with that phrase.

The weather became mild during the week after Christmas and it was drizzling steadily on Wednesday morning when the post arrived. No sooner had the pile of letters been dumped on the ledge by the back door than we heard a familiar roar in the lane outside the house. There had been a general drift towards the kitchen to see what the postman had brought but the Jays, forgetting the letters in their excitement, yelled with one voice, 'It's Darcy!'

They tore out into the driveway and, sure enough, there was the familiar high bonnet of Bertha the Bentley, the flared mudguards and the deep drumming from the exhaust. Darcy switched off the engine and swung his long legs on to the ground.

'What on earth are you doing here?' Jacky asked.

'Well, dig my crazy cousin,' replied Darcy, who prided himself on keeping abreast with modern idioms. 'That's a warm welcome, I must say!'

'Oh, we're glad to see you,' said the diplomatic Jane. 'It's just that we weren't expecting you, that's all.'

'I rang Pat last night,' he explained, 'and told her I had a few days' leave. She invited me down but, dash it all, if I'm not wanted, I've got other places to go.' He pretended to look hurt and made a gesture towards getting back into the car.

'Pat, why didn't you tell us Darcy was coming?' Jacky turned to me.

'Give me a chance,' I said. 'I've only seen you for about quarter of an hour this morning and during that time you've all talked so much that I couldn't have got a word in edgeways! Anyway now you know Darcy's here, let's get him indoors before we're all drenched. Welcome to Miserden, Darcy, in spite of the wet reception!'

'Some people don't have to go out into the rain to get wet,' Jimmy remarked pointedly, with a withering look at Jane and Jacky. He was at an age when an enthusiasm for high-powered machinery was beginning to struggle with his love of horses and he had a special, though private, feeling for Darcy who was a crack pilot in a high-speed squadron testing experimental jets. I noticed that he was the first to grab Darcy's bag and lug it indoors and when Darcy gave him a casual pat on the shoulder in thanks, he went red with pleasure.

Darcy was soon installed in the drawing-room where a log fire blazed on the open hearth. We managed to squeeze another cup of coffee out of the breakfast pot for him and soon we were all chattering and laughing away, reminiscing over our last meeting when Penny Mills had so excitingly won the Ladies' Race at the Ballymulligan Point-to-Point and the Jays had nearly caused an international incident in their escapades over the border between Northern Ireland and Eire.*

During a lull in the conversation, I happened to put a hand in the pocket of my jeans and felt the sharp corner of an envelope. I pulled it out and said 'This might be interesting. It's got your school crest on the flap, Jane and Jacky. I wonder why they should write to you in the holidays.'

'Maybe they want to expel the two girls,' Jimmy commented hopefully. 'It's about time they caught up with them.'

I tore open the envelope and pulled out the letter which was duplicated. I already knew what it would say—after all, Paddy and I had helped to draft it—but I went through the motions of reading it. Then, without a word and trying to keep a straight face, I tossed it over to Jane and Jacky. I watched their faces as they read it and the changes of expression they registered would have won a prize at an actors' school—first surprise, then sheer disbelief and finally awe mingled with excitement.

Jacky breathed out the one word, 'Gosh!' and Jane said, 'It's not a leg-pull, is it, Pat?'

I replied, 'I can't think so. It must be official—with the school crest on the flap.'

'What gives?' Jimmy asked, looking at each of our faces in turn.

I explained the situation. 'It's a letter from Miss Spencer, their headmistress. Any girl in their form who wants to can go in for an essay competition on the subject of why

* See *Three Jays Over the Border.*

Rome is known as the Eternal City. The prize for the best four essays will be to spend about ten days in Rome during the first half of September.'

'But that coincides with the Olympic Games,' Jimmy burst out. 'Boy, what a prize to win! I wish they'd do something like that at my school.'

'Not a hope,' Jacky said smugly. 'You've got to be a vulture for culture before you can appreciate a place like Rome.'

'A fat lot you care for culture!' he retorted. 'The only reason you want to go is to watch the show jumping at the Olympics. Anyway, you won't write one of the four best essays—unless there are only five in your form and one of them's got a broken wrist!'

Jane had been sitting quietly during their exchange and now she looked straight at me and said, 'You're mixed up in this, aren't you, Pat? That visit you paid to Miss Spencer last week—I bet you cooked it up with her then.'

'That had something to do with it,' I admitted. 'She told me how interested you two had suddenly got in the classics—and one thing led to another, you know.'

It was Jane's and Jacky's turn to go red. 'Beast!' Jacky muttered.

'Well, you were obviously angling for a trip to Rome —not in August because it's far too hot then to walk all round the famous churches and monuments but during the first half of September,' I mimicked. 'Of course, it would just be a coincidence that the Olympic Games would be on then. Mind you, it took Miss Spencer in at first but I think she would have rumbled you pretty soon. Who did you say your favourite poet was, Jacky?—was it Virgil, or maybe Horace? No, all I did was to suggest the idea be put on a business-like basis.'

Jane and Jacky glanced ruefully at one another. Then Jacky saw the funny side, said, 'She knows, you know,' and started to giggle. In a moment Jane too went off into a trill of laughter.

Jimmy must have felt that he had been left out of the joke too long. 'What about me?' he demanded. 'I'd like to get to Rome as well as them. Can't you take me along, Pat?'

'I only wish I could but I shan't know whether I'm in the team or not until a month or so before the Games. If I'm not picked for the team, I'd take you like a shot but it'd probably be too late by then to make arrangements.'

'You're bound to be in the team,' he said loyally.

'Hey, not so fast!' I exclaimed. 'There are plenty of people to choose from. Besides, anything can happen—a horse can go lame at the crucial moment or a rider can be off form. If only you three Jays were the selectors—then I'd have no cause to worry!'

Darcy had remained silent all this time, quietly watching the rest of us. Now he emptied his coffee cup, set it down carefully in its saucer on a nearby side table and said, 'I've got an idea, Jimmy. I reckon you may be able to hit Rome without having to write an essay about it.'

Jimmy swung round with eyes and mouth wide open.

'It's like this,' Darcy went on slowly, relishing the moment of suspense. 'The Air Ministry seem to think I've done enough of this high-speed testing for the time being— or will have done when the summer's over. They reckon I'm getting too long in the tooth for all this zooming around the sky like an intrepid aviator....'

'Yes, you are getting a bit ancient,' his cousin Jacky chipped in.'

'Quiet, brat—let the man say his piece,' Jimmy shot at her.

'... Where was I before that unseemly interruption took place?' Darcy grinned.

'Zooming round the sky like an intrepid something or other,' Jane suggested.

'Oh, yes. Anyway, I'll probably leave the squadron and be posted back to General Duties. But I'll have a spot of leave to come to me—to brace myself for the strain of doing some real work for a change! And it could be that Bertha and I might find ourselves driving in the direction of Rome round about the end of August. And if you happened to find yourself wanting a lift thataway, Jim, me lad, well, dash it all, that'd be just mighty fine, pardner, mighty fine.'

'Boy, oh boy!' Jimmy breathed. 'You're a real brick, Darcy! You wouldn't mind if I went with Darcy, Pat, would you?'

'Not as long as he drives carefully and this time remembers that on the Continent the speed limits are worked in kilometres and not miles per hour, I said. This was a dig at our flying friend who, as readers of *Three Jays on Holiday* may recall, once had a brush with a mobile policeman in France because he thought that the sign of a red circle with the figures '60' inside it, on the outskirts of a village, meant that he could drive through the place at sixty miles an hour.

'But that's not really fair. We have to work flat out during the holidays writing an essay—and even then can't be sure of doing one of the best four—while Jim gets to Rome in any case,' Jacky protested.

'Bertha's got a spare seat for stragglers, if you know what I mean,' Darcy said quickly. 'If one of you misses the school bus literally, I can always take her along.'

'But you mustn't bank on that,' I cut in. 'I want you both to try your hardest and win your place on that Dormobile fairly and squarely, if you can. And, as for you, Jim, you needn't think you're getting away with it and not have to work for your trip to Rome. There's no reason why you shouldn't write an essay of your own. Paddy and I can mark it.'

29

'You think of everything, Pat—worse luck!' and he gave a rueful grin.

'Just one point for all of you,' I said, 'before we break it up and get on with some riding.' Darcy squirmed in his chair at the very mention of the word. 'This essay competition is not just a way of keeping you out of mischief during the Christmas holidays. Rome really is a wonderful city and in their way there are no finer sights in the world than the Colosseum standing there at the top of the Via dei Fori Imperiali—or the Trevi Fountain lit up at night. But when I first visited Rome, I knew next to nothing about its historical background and I missed an awful lot. It's only since I began to understand that side that I have begun to appreciate Rome properly. So there's every reason why you ought to read up all you can about it and get some thoughts down on paper.'

'The best sight I can think of is the Olympic Stadium with the Union Jack high on the centre mast after the show jumping team event, and gold medals being dished out to the three of you,' was the irrepressible Jacky's contribution.

'Well, you won't have even the possibility of seeing that unless you produce a proper essay,' I said.

Jane's practical mind was already getting to grips with the problem. 'We'll need to mug up a lot of books on Rome, you know, Pat,' she said. 'I don't suppose we've got any of the ones mentioned in Miss Spencer's letter right here in the house.'

'No, but there are libraries and bookshops in Cheltenham and Gloucester,' I answered. 'Anyway, I've got quite a good guidebook upstairs in my room. You could start on that and, if you write out a list of the others you need, either Paddy or I could get hold of them next time we're in Cheltenham.'

'Do I have to write an essay as well, Pat, to qualify for the trip?' Darcy asked with a twinkle.

30

'I didn't know you could write,' Jacky said.

'You can help Jimmy,' I told him. 'He may need all the help he can get!'

*   *   *

I must say one thing for the essay competition. Whatever its effect on improving the Three Jays' liberal education, it certainly kept them quiet for many hours during the Christmas holidays. They spent every day with pony club rallies, hunting and, in between times, up in the paddock working their ponies or going out for treks across the banks. Once or twice they rode over to Penny Mills's home and helped her exercise Lostboy whom she was hunting regularly and eventually hoped to train into a show jumper. But as soon as the light began to go—or if it was too wet for much riding in the daytime—they would get down to their work for the competition. There was a blessed peacefulness about Miserden House at such times, which it rarely knew when the Jays were in residence.

The closing date for the prize essays was 31st January, just under a fortnight after school reassembled for the Easter term. Jane aimed to have hers done by the time they went back, because she had had the bright idea to borrow Paddy's typewriter and type the essay out neatly. There was nothing in the rules to say that each entry must be handwritten. Jacky, not to be outdone, decided that she too would type hers out, although, as Jimmy quickly pointed out, she typed about as well as a 'drunken monkey.' He decided not to be left behind, so we had to draw up a definite roster for using the typewriter. (If any of my correspondents who failed to receive replies to their letters during that January ever read this book, they will know the reason why! Paddy rarely got the chance of using her own machine.) Darcy, who stayed about a week with us, took the whole business quite seriously. On one occasion I walked quietly into the drawing-room to get a flamenco record and found him deep in an earnest discussion with Jimmy on Etruscan art and its effect on Michelangelo!

The days slid by and, before we knew where we were, the Christmas holidays were almost at an end. It so happened that both Jimmy's school and the girls' school were to reassemble on the same day and I arranged to drive all three of them to Cheltenham, where Jimmy could catch a train for the rest of his journey. Darcy had had to return to his squadron after a week of Christmas leave but he managed to slip away for a half-day on the afternoon before the Jays went back. He joined us at Miserden just before tea-time and right away I seemed to notice an air of conspiracy between Jimmy and himself. Judging by their winks and suppressed laughter, they were enjoying some private joke and I was not reassured when, shortly after the tea things had been cleared away and we were all sitting round the fire in the drawing-room, Jimmy asked gravely if I would like to read his essay on Rome, the Eternal City.

'Of course, I'd love to,' I replied. 'I wondered when you were going to bring the subject up.'

He ran up to his room to fetch it. Darcy meanwhile was staring at the plaster mouldings on the ceiling, with his long legs stretched out towards the log fire. He was smiling to himself and whistling an unrecognizable tune.

'What's the joke, Dashitall?' Jacky demanded. 'Let's all share it.'

'No joke. I was just wondering what you'd think of Jimmy's piece. It's really quite remarkable, I reckon.'

'The remarkable thing is that he's written it at all,' was Jane's retort. 'That is, if he has actually done an esssay. He's been so mysterious about it and wouldn't show it to Jacky or me.'

'Maybe he thought you might crib some of his brilliant

B

ideas,' Darcy said airily—and then flung up his arms in self-protection as the girls began to pelt him with cushions.

As order was restored, Jimmy came back with several sheets of type-written paper stapled together. 'Here you are, Pat,' he said.

'Read it aloud, Pat, then we can all have a good laugh,' Jacky suggested.

I glanced at the first few lines, opened my eyes wider in surprise and then began to read the first page to the others. 'We must understand Dante's words in his *Convivio* that the stones of the walls of Rome deserve reverence, and that the ground on which the city is built is more worthy than men say. Petrarch also gives evidence of a taste divided between classical and Christian antiquity. He tells us how often with Giovanni Colonna he ascended the mighty vaults of the Baths of Diocletian, and there in the transparent air, amid the wide silence, with the broad panorama stretching far around them, they spoke of the history which the ruins beneath their feet suggested. Petrach appeared in their dialogues as the partisan of classical, Giovanni of Christian, antiquity; then they would discourse of philosophy and of the inventors of the arts. How often since that time, down to the days of Gibbon and Niebuhr, have the same ruins stirred men's minds to the same reflections! '

I paused at the end of that impressive paragraph and there was an awestruck silence in the room. During the hush I skimmed my eyes over the rest of the essay, in the hope that sooner or later it would sound like the Jimmy we all knew. But not a bit. It went on in the same vein for several pages, with airy referenres to the 'Rome of the schismatic and Avignonese Popes' and even with footnotes on characters I had personally never heard of such as Gregorovius, Poggio and Fabroni. I looked up from the essay and caught Jimmy's gaze. He stared at me innocently. Darcy was still regarding the ceiling, as though he had only just realized it was there.

Jacky was the first to break the silence. 'You never wrote that by yourself, Jim,' she accused. 'I bet Darcy helped you!'

Darcy said, 'Me? You flatter me, Jacky! I may have gone over his notes with him but I swear I never wrote a word of that. Does it sound like my way of writing?'

'It doesn't a bit,' Jane said quickly. 'Nor does it sound like my dear brother's work either. "Discourse of Philosophy", indeed! You never thought of a phrase like that, Jim!'

'Are you accusing me of cheating?' was the lofty query that came from Jimmy, who still managed to look blankly innocent. The effect was rather spoiled when the two girls said in chorus, 'You bet!'

It was about time, I felt, to investigate the source of this phenomenal essay. 'Jimmy,' I said, 'I don't want to insult you but you must admit that you don't normally write in that way. How do you account for it?'

'There's such a thing as inspiration, you know, Pat,' he answered reproachfully.

Darcy added, 'Don't forget either, Pat, that Jimmy's read a lot of learned books lately. Maybe some of their style has rubbed off on him.'

'Maybe several sentences and even paragraphs have rubbed off, too,' was Jane's nasty suggestion.

For perhaps another five minutes Jimmy kept up the verbal sparring match. I noticed he never claimed definitely that he had written the whole essay by himself and that, when he appeared to be trapped right in a corner, Darcy would come to his rescue with some typically outrages excuse. Perhaps we would never have got to the bottom of it if Paddy, who had gone upstairs again after tea, had not come back to the drawing-room in the middle of the argument.

She looked quizzically at the flushed faces of the Jays

and then said, 'Sorry to butt in—but I've just been collecting up the various books we borrowed from the libraries. I thought you might hand them back when you drive over to Cheltenham tomorrow, Pat. The snag is, there seems to be one missing. I definitely remember we had it a week or so ago but I can't find it anywhere.'

'Do you happen to know the title, Paddy?' I asked.

She fished a list out of her pocket and looked at it. 'Yes, here it is—the only one I haven't ticked off. It's called *The Civilization of the Renaissance in Italy* and it's by somebody named Burckhardt.'

And then the penny dropped with a metaphorical clang. I stared straight at Jimmy, who held my gaze for a second or two and then lowered his eyes and went red. Darcy broke off his unmelodious whistling and began to guffaw loudly. Jimmy joined in and soon the two of them were shaking with helpless laughter.

'That's it,' I said. 'Of course, I see it all now. Petrach and Poggio indeed! Paddy, if you want to find that missing book by Mr. Burckhardt, I suggest you start looking in Jimmy's room.'

'Well, it was a good joke while it lasted,' Darcy commented. 'Pat, you ought to have seen the look on Jane's face while you were reading out all about the mighty vaults of the Baths of Diocletian!'

'You cheat,' Jane said bitterly to her brother. 'I really thought you'd written it yourself at first.'

'I didn't—I guessed there was something fishy about it,' came from Jacky. 'As John Joe Paddy used to say, what can you expect from a pig but a grunt?'

Our Miserden 'pig' put a hand in his jacket pocket and pulled out some folded sheets of paper. 'Just in case you lot didn't know enough classics to follow my serious essay,' he said, 'I did write another simpler one.' Jimmy handed me the pages, which I read aloud to the others. They gave a brief account of the history of Rome from its founding to the present day and showed how Rome had survived several major wars. It was quite a good essay for a young boy and it certainly sounded more like the Jimmy we all knew than the 'deathless prose' he had lifted from Professor Buckhardt as a leg-pull.

'That's not at all bad, Jim,' I said to him, when I had finished reading out his effort. 'I'd say that qualifies you for a trip to the Eternal City. We can even forgive you pulling our legs like that. Do you agree?' I asked the girls.

Jacky nodded grudgingly and Jane went so far as to admit that Jimmy's essay was quite a good effort but she rather spoiled the effect by adding, '—for an ignorant boy!'

'You sound so superior,' Jimmy retorted. 'How about reading out your load of tripe and let's all have a real laugh.'

Jane, nothing daunted, was about to run upstairs and fetch her essay but Jacky looked worried and put out a restraining hand. 'Wait a sec,' she said. 'There's just one thing, Pat. I haven't quite finished mine yet—I've got about another couple of pages to type out which I thought I'd finish off tonight if Paddy'll lend me her typewriter. Miss Spencer did say in her letter that everyone who went in for the competition mustn't get any assistance, apart from reading books on the subject. Jane and I have been careful not to read each other's notes or discuss what we're going to say—just in case we accidentally picked up an idea from the other one. If I'd finished off my own essay completely, I'd love to hear what Jane has written but at the moment I'd rather not, if you know what I mean.'

'That's fair enough, Jacky,' I said. 'You're absolutely right, don't you all agree?' I added, turning to the others.

'Jacky could go upstairs and sit in the cold while we hear what Jane wrote,' Jimmy suggested. 'That way, she wouldn't risk being contaminated with any good ideas—not that my sister is likely to have any!'

In the end it was Jimmy who had to take temporary refuge upstairs, where he was pursued by two determined young women out for vengeance. Luckily for him, he was saved by the bell—the supper-bell.

* * *

A few weeks before Christmas I had taken up an appointment for writing regularly for a national newspaper. Two or three days after I had driven the Jays back to school for the Easter term, I had to fly over to Switzerland and write some articles on the ski-ing championships, the results of which would help the British selectors to chose a team to represent the country at the Winter Olympic Games, to be held at Squaw Valley in the United States Ski-ing has long been one of my favourite sports and I quickly discovered that it had at least one painful thing in common with riding. If you didn't keep your balance at the crucial moment, you could have the whale of a painful fall! I also knew several experts who were likely to be chosen for the team and so I spent a glorious week or so, reporting the events, renewing old friendships and whenever the opportunity could be squeezed in, slipping away up the mountains and getting in some practice of my own. The sun sparkled off the snow and the air was as crisp as a dry white wine. I flew back to London at the end of my visit, feeling fit and refreshed, ready for the gruelling show jumping season that lay ahead.

Paddy met me with the car at London Airport and, as we drove home to Miserden, she reminded me that I was due to give a talk on show jumping that very evening to some of the girls at Jane's and Jacky's school. I had remembered there was some special reason for me to re-

turn home that particular day and not take a short holiday in Switzerland after the ski-ing championships were
over but the crowded hours of the past week had driven
the details from my mind. Fortunately, show jumping is
a subject so close to my heart that I needed little time in
which to prepare a talk on it. For the rest of the drive
back, I used Paddy as a tame audience of one and spoke
my thoughts aloud while she occasionally cut in with a
helpful suggestion or reminded me of an anecdote that
might interest the girls.

Back at Miserden I just had time to read quickly the
more important letters that had arrived in my absence,
check up on the horses, bath, change and try to wash off
some of the sun-tan when it was time to drive on to
Cheltenham. I arrived a minute or two before the talk
was due to begin and barely had time to shake hands
with Miss Spencer before she ushered me on to the plat-
form of the school hall. She asked me to have coffee with
her afterwards and I noticed that she seemed preoccupied, even rather worried, which was unlike her usual
brisk and competent air. I had no time to dwell on
thought, as I needed the last few moments for running
through my mental notes on the talk I was about to give,
and I dismissed it with the feeling that anyone would
look a shade harassed if they had to cope with several
hundred girls at any one time!

The talk seemed to go down quite well, although I was
rather put out of my stride at the start by spotting Jacky
and Jane sitting in the second row. The audience was
composed of older girls from the senior forms and I wondered how the Jays had been able to wangle a place for
themselves at a function held long after their official bed
time. All the same, they behaved with unusual decorum
and didn't laugh before I got to the climax of my stories,
most of which they already knew by heart. I spoke for
about half an hour and then answered questions for

almost as long again. Finally, Miss Spencer wound up the meeting with a brief word of thanks and then whisked me away to her sitting room for coffee. I was just able to wave to the Jays and say, 'See you soon,' but was given no time for a chat with them. I decided ruefully that I was glad not to have to live my whole life at Miss Spencer's quick pace, with apparently every hour of the day—and even every minute of each hour—planned and filled efficiently. I would like to have 'time to stand and stare', as the poet put it, but I realized that one could hardly run a big school on such lines.

It had been a long day, what with flying back from Switzerland, driving nearly a hundred miles to Miserden and then on again, after a brief pause, to Cheltenham, and I was content to relax in an armchair while Miss Spencer bustled about and prepared the coffee in a percolator on a side table. At length, she brought the cups over, poured the coffee and sat down opposite me by the cheerful fire. She still seemed preoccupied and I was quite happy to sit there without talking.

She suddenly came out with, 'Do you mind if I call you Pat? I always think of you by your Chrisian name.'

'Of course,' I said. 'Please call me Pat.'

'Thank you. I'm so glad you managed to come over here tonight, Pat. I particularly wanted to discuss a problem with you.'

Heavens, here we go, I thought, being in no special mood for discussing problems. However, I managed to hide my thoughts and said in a voice that I hoped sounded interested, 'Yes?'

She went on, 'You remember the last time we met and worked out the idea of a trip to Rome for the four girls who wrote the best essays?'

'Of course I remember.'

'Well, Pat, I've marked the essays—Jane's and Jacqueline's are certainly two out of the best four . . .'

'Why, that's marvellous!'

'. . . but I'm afraid Jacqueline's is not original. It looks very much as though she has cheated!'

CHAPTER THREE

EXPLANATION AND PREPARATION

I WAS dumbfounded by this thunderbolt. I suddenly had the feeling, which comes to most of us at some time in our lives, that I must have dropped off in a lightning doze and had just dreamed the last few minutes. I shook my head, both to deny the sense of Miss Spencer's words and also to clear my whirling thoughts into some semblance of order.

'I—I just don't believe it,' I stammered. 'Jacky's not a cheat. I know she gets into scrapes now and then but that's just high spirits. Cheating is a cold-blooded business—and Jacky's not that sort at all!'

'I'd have said exactly the same,' Miss Spencer replied. 'But you can't get away from the evidence of the essay itself. Did you read it all, Pat?'

'No, unfortunately I didn't. Jacky hadn't quite finished it when I last spoke to her about it—and she didn't want me to read it in that state.'

'That could be a sign of a guilty conscience,' Miss Spencer said doubtfully.

'I'm sure not. If anything, I thought she was being a shade too scrupulous. Why, that same evening I remember she asked me not to read Jane's essay aloud because she hadn't quite finished hers and she didn't want to pick up any of Jane's ideas, even unconsciously.'

'Perhaps she didn't want to risk you demanding to see her effort, if you read Jane's out first.'

'Oh, that's impossible!' I exclaimed. 'Jacky's not as subtle as that. This trip to Rome means an enormous lot to her but, even so, I just know she wouldn't cheat her way there.'

'I'd agree with you every time,' Miss Spencer said, but still with a faint note of doubt in her voice. 'The trouble is I'm positive—and so is Miss Haywood, her form mistress—that Jacqueline never wrote the essay by herself. I've compared it with compositions she wrote in form last term—and there's just no comparison. It's full of long words that she'd never use in the normal way and the whole style of the sentences and paragraphs is totally different from Jacqueline's style. Why, it sounds more like the manner in which a professor would write! I haven't been able to track down the source yet but I'm positive the essay's been copied out of some learned work on Rome.'

Miss Spencer's last few remarks touched a faint chord in my memory. 'Have you got the essay handy?' I asked. 'I'd like to read it for myself.'

'Yes, it's over here,' she said, and went over to a table where she rummaged among a neat pile of papers. She brought back several sheets of paper clipped together. The top sheet bore a typed legend—'Why Rome is known as The Eternal City', and several spaces underneath the title, also typed, were the words—'by Jacqueline de Vere Field.'

'You see,' she pointed out, 'there's no mistake. It's got Jacqueline's name on it, clearly enough.'

I nodded and turned the top sheet. My eyes skimmed the first few lines of the essay itself and then I flung my head back and began to laugh helplessly. Miss Spencer must have thought I had suddenly gone stark, staring mad.

'This is not an especially humorous situation, Pat,' she said sharply.

43

'It would be if you knew the full story,' I said, still laughing. I glanced again at the opening paragraph with its mention of Dante and Petrarch and Giovanni Colonna and its phrases like 'the mighty vaults of the Baths of Diocletian'. 'This isn't Jacky's essay at all.'

'That's what I've been saying all along,' was her severe comment.

'No I don't mean it that way, Miss Spencer. Please let me explain.' I went on to tell her how Jimmy, whom she remembered from an earlier occasion when Jane and Jacky had been accused of copying off each other in an exam,* had pulled our legs with Darcy's help by copying out some extracts from a learned tome by a Swiss professor named Burckhardt and pretending that he had written it by himself. 'That's the same paper and typing,' I went on, 'I'd recognize it anywhere. Look, here's where he started to type a word wrongly, x-ed it out and typed it over again. I distinctly recall that same mistake in the copy Jimmy showed me a couple of weeks ago.'

'If that's so, how do you account for the fact that it has Jacqueline's name clearly typed on the title page?'

I thought hard for a moment. 'How does Jacky usually describe herself?' I asked. 'As Jacqueline Field—or with her full name written out?'

It was Miss Spencer's turn to pause and think. 'Usually just Jacqueline Field,' she said at last.

'I thought so,' I said and then looked quickly at my wrist-watch. 'I might catch him now,' I added, half to myself, and then said to Miss Spencer 'Could I possibly use your phone? One call might clear up all this nonsense.'

She nodded and I asked for the number of Darcy's R.A.F. station. Luckily, he was in the Officers' Mess and

* See *Three Jays Go to Town.*

his well-known tones came booming down the line from over fifty miles away. I asked him point-blank if he and Jimmy had carried out a leg-pull on Jacky by typing out a fresh title page in her name to the cribbed essay and slipping it in with her school things on the evening before she returned to school. Darcy hummed and hawed a little but when I urged him to tell me the real facts and help Jacky not to be wrongly blamed, he admitted it all.

'Dash it all, Pat,' he said protestingly, 'we never meant to get Jacky into trouble. We thought she'd be bound to read the essay over before she handed it in. Besides, her own essay was just underneath the spoof one. We reckoned she'd be certain to wonder why there were two essays in the one folder.'

'Knowing Jacky, she probably handed it in in a last-minute rush and never stopped to see what she was doing,' I said. I added severely, 'Anyway, Darcy, it was a pretty stupid and dangerous sort of leg-pull. You might have got her into serious trouble. Jimmy's too young to look ahead to the consequences of a practical joke like that— but there's no excuse for you.'

'I'm terribly sorry, Pat,' he said in a contrite tone. 'Dash it all, I really am sorry. We never dreamed there'd be any comeback. Is there any thing I can do to put it right?'

'Yes—have a word with Miss Spencer, Jacky's headmistress, who's right behind me now. Explain it all to her. She might accept your apology.'

I handed the receiver to Miss Spencer and privately guessed what would happen. She began by talking with a frosty edge to her voice but gradually thawed out as Darcy, who could be persuasively charming when he tried, started to explain the situation. Towards the end of their conversation, she even chuckled once or twice and she bade him good night quite warmly when she finally hung up.

'What an entertaining young man he seems to be,' she said. 'I understand it all now. He and Jane's brother only meant to play a joke on Jacqueline.'

'Oh, sure,' I answered. 'No malice aforethought at all. It's just their sense of humour that I don't find very funny.'

'You mustn't be hard on them, Pat,' she said. 'After all, people do reckless things when they are young.'

I privately thought that now I had heard everything. I had begun by explaining Darcy to her and now she was ending up by defending him against me! Anyway, he appeared to have pulled Jacky out of the scrape into which he and Jimmy had thoughtlessly pushed her, so, as Miss Spencer had suggested, I 'mustn't be hard on him'. G-r-r-r-r!

She cut my thoughts by saying, 'Well, that settles that. I should have realized that Jacqueline is not the kind of girl to cheat and I ought really to have looked harder for the right solution. I expect her real essay is still lying in her case—we must arrange for her to collect it first thing in the morning. Good heavens, Pat, the coffee's gone quite cold with all these false alarms! Let me ring for some fresh coffee, won't you?

But I asked her not to worry on my account. All I wanted was to drive home to Miserden, drop into bed and forget Darcy, the school, essay competitions—and even the Jays—for the next six hours. It had been quite a day!

* * *

Spring arrived all too quickly in this Olympic year. Winter gave one dying kick by producing blizzards, rain and the worst floods that the Severn Valley had known for years but we, on the high, rolling 'banks' of Gloucestershire, were safe from any flood-water. Then the days began to lengthen almost magically, thrushes sang or hopped about in courting pairs and the crocuses pushed up their

46

silent trumpets to herald the spring and join the legions of aconites and snowdrops already waiting for them.

During the second half of February, I was lucky enough to get a foretaste of summer by flying to South Africa and taking part in the show jumping championships in the Cape. I had the greatest fun jumping horses that I had never seen before, lent to me by kind people for various competitions. On the first day the horses all co-operated to win me all four competitions. Apart from the jumping I was taken to various parts of the beautiful country around the Cape. I saw some of the farms where the thoroughbreds are raised and I admired their wonderful condition and their lovely surroundings of mauve mountains rising out of the plain. The grape harvest had just started and the coloured workers in the vineyards were filling baskets with ripe bunches of grapes and then tipping them into the trailers which were then taken to the presses by tractor. In the buildings, even the boss's six-year-old son was helping to unload the grapes, and I was shown the whole process to the stream of grape juice pouring into huge tanks, where the wine would ferment. Another day I was taken in a launch to Seal Island which has thousands of seals living on the rock together with some penguins. Some of the sea-lions were fighting between themselves and did not take any notice of our boat passing by.

I was enchanted by the country but time waits for no one and I had one more port of call before the Olympic training began. After the championships had finished I left the Cape and flew home by Comet. Soon I was off again, this time to Switzerland, for a last brief ski-ing holiday and a visit to the Davos Horse Show, although I had no horses. Flanagan and Carousel between them had won the Prix du Parsenn for the past three years there, and this time I was invited to build the course, judge and present the prizes for this competition. It was quite a

47

change from competing myself. Meanwhile I was getting as fit as possible by a different form of arduous and exciting sport—ski-ing. There were many months of hard work ahead for both the horses and myself and even after the culminating point of the Olympic Games there was to be yet another European tour behind the Iron Curtain. With this busy year ahead I really enjoyed the few days in the mountains.

On my return I spent the rest of March getting the horses fit to go to Arundel for the beginning of the Olympic training programme. I had two shows as a pipe opener for the horses before we arrived in our Sussex quarters at the beginning of April. The Duke of Norfolk had generously put the wonderful facilities of Arundel Park at the disposal of the British Show Jumping Association, together with the services of Colonel Talbot-Ponsonby, in charge of the horsy side of the establishment, who had trained the Olympic Team in 1956 and was to do so again this year. Seven riders, each with their chosen horses, had been nominated for special training. From their showing during the month of April and from the results they would achieve at certain specially selected International Horse Shows and national demonstrations during the following two or three months, the final Olympic Team would be chosen.

The Jays had still a week or so of the Easter term to finish when Paul and I, accompanied by the two horses, drove off to Arundel in the horse-box. I was sorry to miss them, particularly as we had seen little of each other during term-time, but the training-course only went on during week-days and I would be able to get home to Miserden each week-end. Indeed, I felt rather ruefully that my term was starting just as their finished.

My second week-end at home coincided with the Jay's return from school and we had a boisterous reunion. I soon learned that the efficient Miss Spencer had just about completed all the plans for the trip to Rome. Luckily, Jacky's real essay had proved to be one of the best four in her class and so she had won her seat in the Dormobile (which a friend of mine had kindly agreed to lend the school for a nominal sum) along with Jane and two other girls named Margaret and Valerie. I never discovered their surnames or, if the Jays did tell me, I must have forgotten them. Miss Haywood, their form mistress, was to be in charge of the party and another mistress named Mark was the spare driver and 'whipper-in', as the hunting-minded Jimmy put it. The party was to assemble in London on 25th August, cross the Channel to France next day and drive by easy stages to Rome. I was glad to see that the route took in such famous places as Versailles, Fontaine-bleau and Chartres but I secretly wondered just for how long the two girls would stand up to what Jimmy would call being 'culture-vultures'. Anyway, if only a vague memory remained in their minds afterwards of the stately elegance of Versailles or the radiant rose-window of Chartres, it would enrich them.

Meanwhile Jimmy and Darcy had not been idle over their own plans, I gathered. Owing to the rush on ferry-bookings, they had been unable to arrange their crossings on the same ship as the girls. Instead Darcy had booked on the air-ferry from Lydd in the afternoon of the same day. This would put them several hours behind the Dor-mobile but Darcy relied on his trusty old Bentley to make up the time by the second day. I reminded Jimmy and told him to pass the word on to his older colleague that this was to be no joy-ride on their part. The rules of the game were that they also should stop at all the various cultural spots on the route and I threatened to give them an oral examination on reaching Rome, just to make sure that they had taken everything in. Jimmy's face fell nearly a yard at this reminder. There were times when anything over twenty years old struck him as too 'square' for words and, as he said to me, 'I don't dig these old ruins. If they weren't good enough to keep in repair, then let 'em moulder away without my help!' It was not worth arguing with him and pointed out that the magnificent cathedrals that they would see, like Chatres, were hardly 'old ruins' but are in daily use. He would find out for himself soon enough!

One other thing I discovered on my return to Miserden that week-end. Jacky had persuaded Paddy to organize a day's outing for the three of them at Arundel, where they wanted to watch me train with the rest of the riders. They had had enough coaching out of me over the years and now I suspected they would enjoy seeing the boot on the other foot. It was roughly one hundred and thirty miles from Miserden to Arundel and the idea was for Paddy and the Jays to start out very early in the morning and drive down, stay until the early afternoon and then go back via London where they would spend the night in the large flat belonging to Jacky's father. Jacky had indeed planned everything out. She had telephoned her busy father and had even wheedled him into agreeing to take them out and see a show that evening. Next morning they would drive back to Miserden. The day they had chosen was the Wednesday of the following week.

Luckily, it was a bright, crisp spring morning when they all arrived in the car, having stopped for breakfast on the road.

I had told them how to get to the training ground in the Park and sure enough they were sitting in the car when I rode up at 9 a.m. I think that they had been a bit overawed by the sight of the grand castle with its towers, moat, drawbridge and portcullis, but as soon as they saw me they tumbled out of the car and came running across the wet grass to greet me. 'We practically left Miserden by moonlight,' shouted Jacky.

'Thanks to me hauling you out of bed, Miss Field,

50

otherwise we wouldn't have made Arundel before twilight,' Jane commented. I congratulated Paddy on arriving with the family so early, and told them that they could look at the lovely fences, ditches and banks while we were working the horses.

Jumping was not started until half past nine and then each of the riders would work one horse over the fences as organized by our team trainer, Colonel Jack Talbot-Ponsonby. That morning the five of us that were present were going to jump only our first horses, those most likely to be in the final selection, in this No. 1 arena. The ground was still very wet from heavy overnight rain. We did not want to cut up the turf in this arena, so after jumping our first horses we were going to work the rest of the horses over another set of fences at the far end of the park.

Each of us rode to various corners of the surrounding park taking care to walk carefully over the gallops for the race-horses. It was essential that we did not make a track by crossing the gallops in the same place each day. The turf was kept in beautiful condition on the gallops and peat had been spread over them. The new grass had started to come through the peat, ensuring springy going all through the summer, even if there was no rain.

I selected a place with tufty grass near the Hiorne Tower where I could school Flanagan in circles. He was very fresh to start with but I let him have a scamper around and one or two little cat-bucks to work off his high spirits. His activities made him breathe deeply and he coughed a couple of times, but then he blew his nose too, so I knew he was only clearing his wind and not sickening with a cough.

After a few minutes I pulled him up and made him rein back. He realized that I wanted him to work properly now, because he had already had a half-hour's walk up to the arena and so was ready to begin some collected cantering and change of pace between the canter and trot. He went into his work quite readily as he had been in training for a little time and had settled down well.

Meantime Colonel Talbot-Ponsonby had arrived in his jeep and was arranging the fences as he wanted them for that morning's jumping. I was pleased to see out of the corner of my eye, that the Jays kept tactfully out of the way and returned to the car. I found out later that they had not wasted their time, as they made a plan of the fences with the distances between any combination of fences. They also had the width and depth of the ditches and the height of the banks. I decided that they did not miss much between them. The double that intrigued them most were the 'bidets'. The poles could be adjusted over the waters to make parallel bars or just straight poles on either side. I had often met this jump abroad but as the Jays had not been to a show outside England, they had no idea about some of the Continental fences.

Brigadier Blacker was the first to jump as he had to return to his military duties at Sandhurst when he had finished. I could not watch Workboy while he was jumping, as I was next on Flanagan and he still needed some circling to get him supple before I jumped him. Workboy was quite hot when he had finished, but none of the un-clipped horses had got their summer coats through yet. Flanagan's coat was pouring out and each time I breathed in I got a mouthful of hair. This stage of the springtime change of coats would not last long, thank goodness. With Paul's constant grooming and the heavy rug he wore in the stable I hoped that his sleek summer coat would be through by the first of the big shows.

That morning I was jumping a course of fences, mostly spreads, to make Flanagan stretch over his fences. He is a short coupled horse and to make up for this he needed practice to make him stretch his head and neck while

52

jumping. A horse with a long back always finds it easier to jump wide fences.

Flanagan enjoyed the course set for him and scampered around finding no trouble with the lines of fences. He cleared the water easily as there was a bar placed over it to make the horse jump higher. He just tapped the last fence, a parallel bars over the narrow green bank, but that was because he was puffed. This was only the beginning of the season and he was not meant to be completely fit yet.

I walked him back to Colonel Talbot-Ponsonby after jumping the last fence and he nodded and said that Flanagan had done enough for today. I rode over to Paul so that he could take Flanagan back to the stables. I passed Ann Townsend, walking Bandit around with David Barker on Franco and David Broome on Wildfire, who were all waiting to see who was next to go.

Paul gave Flanagan some grass as a reward and then took him while I rode on to the other arena of fences with my next horse.

The jumping of our second strings passed uneventfully, but Jimmy was very impressed by a big bay thoroughbred that Colonel Talbot-Ponsonby was riding. I told him that his name was Flamingo Bay and he belonged to the Queen Mother.

When I had finished work that morning, they all came back to the Norfolk Arms and had lunch with me there. I sent them off to London afterwards looking very well fed and sleepy, except for Paddy, who in spite of the long drive in the early morning was her usual bright and energetic self.

*   *   *

Summer seemed to arrive on a long stride. One moment the first training month at Arundel was on and then May,

June and July had been left behind like jumps taken in a speed competition. The International Horse Show at the White City towards the end of July had been the highlight of the English season.

There were five Olympic teams competing there and the United States team beat us in the Nation's Cup. A slight compensation for this was that Great Britain won the King's Cup with David Broome on Sunsalve. I was delighted with my horses, too, as Flanagan won the Prince Hal Stakes in memory of his old stable pal, and also the Country Life & Riding Cup that Hal had won in 1951. I had last ridden Scorchin before the Stockholm Olympics but we renewed our partnership for the White City and he won me the Daily Mail Cup, the final Individual Championship. Prince Hal had won this cup in 1955 and again in 1957 when it proved to be the last International event and triumph of his life. I had been runner-up three times, with Hal in 1951, Tosca in 1952 and Flanagan in 1956, all by a margin of about one fifth of a second in the final jump off. Anyway, dear Scorchin clinched the hattrick.

I saw little enough of the Jays during this time. We did, however, manage to get together at Miserden for the last week-end before they left on their drive to Rome.

When I arrived, the situation was normal—in other words, as Jimmy would say—everything was in 'a state of choss'. Paddy, the methodical one, was upstairs, emptying and putting away four out of the six pigskin suitcases which Jacky had blithely packed to include a change of clothing for every variety of climate from the arctic to the tropical. The first step in any move away from Miserden was tactfully to persuade Jacky to thin out her luggage and so leave just a little space on board the vehicle for other people! Jacky herself was down in the drawing-room, strumming away on an old guitar I had once given her in an unguarded moment. She had a singular gift for picking wrong notes and this was matched by a voice which she fondly thought resembled the tone of the Spanish gipsies but which relied actually on its two qualities of penetrating loudness and complete lack of rhythm!

Undeterred by the strange screechings that emerged from Jacky's end of the room—with a superhuman effort I thought I detected something vaguely resembling the melody of *Arrivederci Roma*—Jimmy and Jane were giggling over an old foreign language phrase-book they had discovered.

'Hey, Pat, listen to this,' Jimmy called out as he saw me come in. 'Pipe down for a second, Jacky, will you? If the R.S.P.C.A. man happened to drive by, he'll think there's a cat being killed in here!'

'What's up, Jimmy?'

'This is wonderful,' he said. 'Do listen. It tells a sad story in half a dozen sentences. These are the bits you need to know if you're travelling by air. It starts off quite happily with "Book me a seat—*Mi prenoti un posto*". Then you get "At what time does the aeroplane start?— *A che ora e la partenza?*". Now the drama begins to creep in. "Steward, please—*Il cameriere per favore*". The next bit goes straight to the crisis. "I am feeling sick— *Ho mal de cuore*". Now things are really tough. "Do you have any paper bags for airsickness?—*Ci sono dei succhetti per il mal d'aria?*"'

'That's odd,' Jane commented. 'I thought *mal d'aria* was the way Jacky sings!'

'No, it's "air-sickness",' Jimmy went on, too absorbed to spot the sarcastic note in her voice. 'Mind you, the next bit could apply to Jacky. "Have you any cotton-wool plugs for my ears?—*Ci sono dei batuffoli di bambagia?*". Then the character obviously recovers a bit, for his next question is "Can one get anything to eat?— *Si puo avere qualcosa da mangiare?*". But he's not too

55

sure of himself because the very last sentence is "When do we land?—*Quando atterreremo*?" What do you think of that, Pat?'

'Words fail me,' I said. 'With your Italian accent, Jim, maybe it's just as well you won't be travelling by air—except from Lydd to Le Touquet.'

Jacky had fortunately put down her guitar and was now peering over Jimmy's shoulder. 'That's what you make me,' she said to him. '*Mal de cuore*—that means "sick"!'

The Jays were obviously well in their usual form of being rude to one another, so I thought it best to divert there verbal energy. 'Are you more or less organized? I asked.

'More less than more,' Jane told me. 'The idea is for Paddy to drive all three of us up to London on Wednesday and we'll spend the night at Jacky's palatial residence. The other two—Val and Margaret—are to meet us there early next morning and so will Miss Haywood and Miss Mark with the Dormobile. Then off we drive to Dover. Darcy can't leave his R.A.F. station until that morning and so Jimmy'll wait behind at the flat for an hour or so until Darcy turns up to collect him. They'll drive down to Lydd—if Bertha holds out that long! We reckon to get a bit south of Paris by Thursday evening. I believe Miss Haywood has looked up the camping spots and there's quite a good one near Fontainebleau.'

'Are you going to camp out as well?' I asked Jimmy. I could see trouble ahead; the two school-mistresses might not altogether appreciate Darcy's and Jimmy's leg-pulling sense of humour on a camping expedition.

'Not us,' he replied. 'We're going to rough it each night in the best hotel we can find! Darcy reckons he's done enough camping to last him a lifetime. Mind you, I'd rather like to take a tent along and sleep under canvas —but he's the boss.'

'You need to be tough—like us—to enjoy camping.' Jacky said to him. 'I doubt if you'd stand up to it, Jim.'

'Tough,' he sneered. 'You call living in that hotel on wheels tough? You ought to see the Dormobile, Pat— they brought it over the other day to work out the sleeping arrangements. The roof has a kind of canvas shelter that opens up and you pull out bunks on the side walls. It's jolly ingenious, I must say, but there's nothing spartan about it. 'Course, they'll need a trailer as well to pull along behind.'

'What for?' asked the unsuspecting Jacky.

'To carry all your luggage, stupid,' came the quick answer.

'Talking of luggage,' I said before Jacky could start a row, 'is all your packing done?'

'Just about,' Jane told me. 'Miss Haywood has rationed us to one large suitcase each, plus a grip for our overnight things. It's hard on Jacky not being able to change for dinner every night on the road but she's been gallant enough to accept the sacrifice!'

'How about changing the record?' asked the long-suffering Jacky. 'Just because you're all jealous of my charm and good looks and wealth—and the fact that I don't have to rely on an old cardboard suitcase with the locks broken, eh, Jimmy?'

Jimmy was as practical as ever. 'You can keep the charm and good looks, so called—I'll just have the wealth any time you've done with it.'

'One thing we're not too sure of, Pat,' Jane said. 'Should we take our swimming things? What's the chance of getting a swim while we're in Rome?'

'In Rome itself—just about nil, I'd say. The Olympic Baths will be kinda busy and I wouldn't recommend the Tiber! But there are some wonderful beaches along the coast less than an hour's drive from Rome. Places like

Fregene and the Rome Lido at Ostia. And there's miles of golden beach stretching all the way down from Ostia to Anzio. The old town of Ostia is pretty interesting—it's got a very well preserved amphitheatre—and you might persuade Miss Haywood to kill two birds with one stone by going there one day, sight-seeing in the morning and having a swim in the afternoon.'

Jacky asked, 'Pat, what's an amphi—whatever you called it?'

'Wait till you've been in Rome a day or two. You'll soon find out! Then I added, I don't want to preach a sermon but do make the most of this opportunity, won't you. Rome isn't just a place where they're going to hold the Olympic Games. They'll be exciting enough, goodness knows, but without them Rome is still a superb city, perhaps the most beautiful one in the world. And it's not merely a show-place, a carefully preserved museum. Life has gone on there continuously for over two thousand years and it's the centre of a great religion as well as a political capital. You don't have to be a Catholic to be impressed by St. Peter's or a Latin scholar to stand in the Colosseum and imagine yourself back in the days of Nero watching the gladiators fight to the death. Rome is a great experience—do get all you can out of it while you're there.'

'Hey, you must have been reading my essay, Pat, the one I pinched out of the book,' was the irrepressible Jimmy's wisecrack.

'Well, having no more pearls to cast, I'll be off to do my own packing,' I snorted. 'See you in Rome—arrivederci.'

'Arrivederci Roma, Pat!' they chorused.

58

CHAPTER FOUR

ALL ROADS LEAD TO ROME

*M*Y next reunion with the Jays was in Rome itself. They took five days to get there, Jacky and Jane travelling with their school party in the Dormobile, Jimmy accompanying Darcy in the old Bentley. I flew there direct—in under five hours 'from door to door'. And so this next chapter, describing their adventures on the road, really comes to you, as the advertisements say, by courtesy of the Jays themselves. It is their story, which I collected by talking to them each in turn and cross-checking the facts with Darcy as well. If I had relied entirely on Jacky's version, the chapter might have been twice as exciting to read but possibly half as accurate into the bargain! Not that Jacky tells untruths, of course. But she is a born dramatist who, when the mood is on her, could make crossing the road sound an adventure to match Sir Vivian Fuchs's crossing of the Antarctic! Anyway, here is the result of my investigations.

* * *

The Dormobile party crossed the Channel without incident—it was luckily a calm day and the sea was like a mill-pond—and after an hour's wait while the vehicles were unloaded and the passengers went through the French Customs, they were bowling merrily southwards towards Paris along the straight, poplar-fringed stretches of the N.1. Jacky and Jane vaguely remembered the road from the time they travelled down it with Darcy in the vintage Bentley. They tried to recall just which village it was where Darcy had had his brush with the mobile policeman for innocently exceeding the speed limit of sixty kilometres an hour. They failed—for French villages have a strange habit of looking alike, with their dun-coloured cottages and no gardens, cobblestones and garish advertisements on the walls for *Pneus Englebert* and the exhortations to bibulous drivers—*Santé, Sécurité, Sobriete*. Nor was Miss Haywood, who took the first two-hours spell at the wheel, likely to emulate Darcy's dash. She drove at a steady, if slightly nervous, thirty-five miles an hour, keeping the Dormobile well tucked in to the right of the road. It was her first experience of driving under Continental conditions and she was taking no risks. Every time a Citroën or a Renault came flashing by with a loud blast on the horn, she drew in nearer to the verge and, as Jacky whispered to Jane sitting alongside her, gave the driver her 'no-marks-for-neatness' look!

Miss Mark, the other mistress, sat in front beside her, studying a Michelin Atlas with *'Grandes Routes FRANCE'* in letters of gold on its blue cover. (When Jimmy had heard that Miss Spencer had agreed to the plan and that someone named Miss Mark was going on the trip, he had immediately christened the project as the 'Marks & Spencer holiday outing'!) Both the grown-ups were taking their duties seriously. When Miss Spencer had first mooted the plan, they had looked on it as a splendid cultural holiday with just a dash of added excitement. Now they had actually started and each of them realized the responsibility of getting themselves and four high-spirited youngsters to Rome and back—over a thousand miles each way through strange territory. Anything

60

might go wrong. Perhaps the Dormobile would break down or one of the girls fall ill. They knew that you couldn't always rely on the drinking water in foreign countries; why, in Italy even the local people whose stomachs must be hardened against bugs drank either wine or aerated water out of bottles. They wanted to be broad-minded and not impose a school atmosphere on what was basically a holiday but each of them wondered privately just how much they could relax the discipline, particularly with the Jays on board. Jane was sensible enough most of the time but Jacky—and here Miss Haywood gave a resigned sigh and gripped the steering-wheel more tightly. Jacky was a fine girl at heart, she realized, but she was both impulsive and accident-prone—the only youngster she had ever taught who could run amok while sitting down! There was no malice in Jacky but she seemed to attract crises like a magnet. Miss Haywood mentally crossed her fingers.

Glancing in the driving-mirror, her eyes caught Valerie and Margaret sitting together. They at least should cause no trouble. Valerie with her long fair curls and big blue eyes was the model schoolgirl. Always neat and tidy, always punctual, always devoted to school word and learning, she seemed almost too good to be true. Why, even now she had a guidebook open on her knees and every time they passed through a village or town she spotted the name and looked up the index to see if there was anything of historical interest to note. She intended to write an article for the school magazine on the tour and had already begun to keep a special diary in which she wrote down her impressions in a neat, clear hand. Margaret had horn-rimmed glasses and a solemn gaze. She was not a talkative girl and she treated everything in a quiet, matter-of-fact way. Miss Haywood often wondered just what went on behind those slightly short-sighted eyes. But at least she knew that the girl was not

61

a harum-scarum tomboy. Thank Heavens for that—and she sighed again, this time with relief. Two Jackies on a trip like this would be at least one too many!

Although Miss Haywood's driving would have given Stirling Moss no grounds for jealousy, the Dormobile made reasonable progress along the rather dull and open roads of Northern France. After a two-hour driving spell, she changed with Miss Mark a few kilometres outside Abbeville. On they went through Beauvais, where Valerie wanted to stop and study the cathedral. She was out-voted. Jacky and Jane reckoned they would see enough cathedrals on the trip without throwing in an extra one. The two seniors, while appreciating Valerie's quest for culture, felt they ought to press on without delay and reach Versailles by the early afternoon. Their plan was to spend an hour or two there and then drive on a further forty miles or so to Fontainebleau where there was a special camping site for cars and caravans.

They had decided in advance to by-pass Paris and its hustling traffic. So, just south of Beauvais while Valerie was still looking pathetic because she had been robbed of an extra paragraph for the school magazine, they turned off on the twisty narrow road leading to Pontoise. They lost their way a couple of times in the country lanes but at last emerged at St. Germain sunning itself by a broad bend in the River Seine. They drove on south-wards, crossed the *autoroute* where the cars whirled by with true Gallic dash and not long afterwards drew up in the broad, cobbled square of Versailles.

Miss Haywood, who had taken over the driving again at St. Germain, managed to squeeze the Dormobile into a convenient gap between the hundreds of cars parked in the square and switched off the engine. One by one the passengers got out and gazed at the great, grey palace that breasted the slope ahead of them.

'Now then, girls,' said Miss Haywood briskly in her

best class-room manner, 'before we inspect it closely, I wonder if any of you can tell the rest of us about the history of this splendid place?'

Jacky caught Jane's eye and twitched her nose in a grimace. They both liked Miss Haywood but they wished she could drop that hearty, 'jolly hockey sticks' approach. This was a holiday trip, not a history lesson back at school.

But the earnest Valerie picked up the cue at once. 'Please, Miss Haywood,' she said, 'I can tell you about it.' She took a deep breath and began her recital. 'The royal palace of Versailles was built at the command of Louis the thirteenth—at least, the central part which we're now facing was built in his reign. His successor, Louis the Fourteenth, known as "Le Roi Soleil" or Sun-King, added the wings on either side of the main part. He also built the Grand Trianon which is a small palace with its own gardens in the park behind the big palace. Louis the Fifteenth built the Petit Trianon, which is another small palace in the park, and Marie-Antoinette, who was later to be guillotined in the French Revolution with her husband Louis the Sixteenth, used the Petit Trianon as a rustic retreat. . . .'

'Dig her,' Jacky whispered to Jane, 'the original walking history book!' '. . . In 1789,' Valerie continued, now well into her stride, 'the National Assembly, who wanted to overthrow the Royal Family, met here in defiance of the king's orders and swore an oath which became known as the Tennis Court Oath because they met secretly in the Tennis Court. . . .'

'I've heard one or two oaths on tennis courts,' Jacky commented innocently.

'Please don't interrupt Valerie, Jacqueline,' said Miss Haywood. 'If you have a question to ask, keep it until she has finished. Do go on, Valerie, this is all most interesting.'

Valerie had heard Jacky's remark and she glared at her before proceeding with, 'I'm sorry, Miss Haywood, it's difficult to concentrate when one is continually being interrupted with facetious comments. Where was I?— oh yes, the Tennis Court Oath. The members of the National Assembly swore that they would not separate until they had drawn up a proper democratic constitution for France. Other important points to note about Versailles are that the Treaty of Paris was signed here in 1783 by which France recognized the independence of the United States of America. After the Franco-Prussian War of 1870 King William of Prussia was proclaimed German Emperor here and, in more recent times, the Treaty of Versailles which laid down the conditions for peace with Germany after the First World War was signed here on the twenty-eighth of June, 1919.'

'That's absolutely splendid, Valerie,' Miss Haywood said with enthusiasm. 'You've obviously taken great pains to read up the history. Well done! Now have any of you others any questions to ask?'

Jacky shot up her hand. Miss Haywood looked surprised. Jacky, she had supposed, was the last person present who would be interested in further historical knowledge. 'Yes, Jacqueline, what is it?' she asked in a kindly tone.

'Please, Miss Haywood, do you think we might buy an ice-cream from the stall over there?' came the question.

As Jane remarked afterwards, the atmosphere suddenly got so cold that no one needed an ice cream. Miss Haywood pursed her lips and shook her head sorrowfully. Such levity in these solemn surroundings was too much for words. She decided to ignore Jacky's frivolity. 'Well,' she said firmly, 'if there are no proper questions, let us now go up to the palace. I believe the Hall of Mirrors is a magnificent sight.'

Margaret, inscrutable behind her thick glasses, asked,

'Is that what they call the Galerie des Glaces, Miss Haywood?'

'Yes, Margaret, I think it is.'

'But I thought *glace* meant an ice-cream?'

'It does, Margaret—but the word has two different meanings. Can any of you think of an English word with two different meanings?'

'Yes,' Jacky butted in, 'the word "ice". One meaning is "frozen water"—the other is "ice-cream"—like those smashing ices they're selling on the stall just a yard or two away!'

Miss Haywood was beginning to lose her temper. 'Jacqueline Field,' she said abruptly, 'You know perfectly well that you cannot go into a palace licking ices. Let us hear no more of the subject.'

She walked ahead up the slope, followed by Miss Mark, Valerie clutching her guidebook and notebook and Margaret, still looking a little dazed. Jane and Jacky brought up the rear and, when they seemed safely out of earshot, Jane remarked, 'Now that's what I call an icy comment!'

They spent an hour studying the palace and even the Jays had to admit that it was a most impressive sight, with its splendid tapestries, lofty rooms, statues and perfectly kept gardens. It was even possible for them to imagine themselves back in the eighteenth century, when Marie-Antoinette and her gay courtiers played at being shepherds and shepherdesses in their make-believe rural world, unmindful that their flocks of peasants outside the walls were slowly preparing to turn and overthrow their frivolity in the blood-stained Revolution that was soon to crash on them.

At one point the party split up. Valerie wanted to go back for another look at the Hall of Mirrors and Miss Mark went with her. The others strolled along the terrace at the rear of the main building, watching the sun dan-

C

cing on the ornamental lake. Jane and Jacky expected a long wait for they knew that if Valerie had one of the seniors as her audience, she would surely try her best to impress her with her historical knowledge. But scarcely ten minutes later, a white-faced Miss Mark came rushing along the terrace, followed by Valerie.

'What's the matter?' Miss Haywood asked with concern. 'Has anything happened?'

Miss Mark replied grimly, Yes, it has. We've just been accosted by a rude young man!'

'Good Heavens, a Frenchman,' Miss Haywood shared the belief that all Frenchmen, young or old, were secret Lotharios at heart

'No, far worse than that. He was English! At least he spoke English. And what makes it seem all the more dreadful, he had a young boy with him.'

Miss Haywood drew her a few paces to one side. 'What actually happened?' she muttered.

Indignation had now taken the place of alarm in Miss Mark's emotions and she spoke loudly enough for the Jays to hear her. 'Valerie and I were standing just inside the Hall of Mirrors, discussing the Treaty of Versailles and why it had never been properly successful. Then suddenly this strange young man appeared in the doorway, followed by the boy. He was a villainous looking creature—the man, I mean—and he kept staring at us. He had a big, red moustache and an evil look in his eyes. He said something to the boy, who started laughing, and then he came over to us and said in a threatening tone, "Mrs. Livingstone, I presume?" Valerie and I were so taken aback we couldn't move for the moment and then we just took to our heels.'

'What a disgraceful business!' Miss Haywood said warmly. Then, as an afterthought, she added, 'I suppose he couldn't have mistaken you for someone he knew?'

'No,' was the firm answer, quite impossible. It was

66

obviously a deliberate attempt to make our acquaintance. Poor Valerie here must have had a great shock—I know I did!'

'Poor Valerie' seemed to the Jays' unfeeling eyes to have recovered promptly from the shock. She looked delighted to be the centre of attraction.

'Ought we to report this to the local police?' Miss Haywood wondered aloud, 'The man may be dangerous, a criminal perhaps or an escaped lunatic.'

Miss Mark was taken aback at the implied suggestion that a man would have to be out of his mind before he tried to make her acquaintance. 'What's the use?' she snapped. 'He may be miles away by now—with his young accomplice.' Then her eyes widened and she flung a hand up to her throat. 'My goodness—here he comes! What are we going to do?'

The others shot round and saw a tall young man threading his way through the visitors on the terrace. He was followed by a boy in his teens and they were quite obviously making a bee-line for the group. Both of them were smiling—at least, the girls could see a smile on the boy's face. The man's ginger handle-bar moustache made it difficult to see his mouth from that range. They were frozen like the statues nearby for a second or two and then Jacky broke the spell. 'It's only Darcy and Jimmy,' she announced. 'Hallo there, Darcy!' and she waved her hand.

'Wotcher', he said, as he came close to them.

*　　*　　*

It took Darcy less than five minutes to smooth down Miss Mark's ruffled plumage. He explained that he and Jimmy, having landed at Le Touquet a couple of hours after the Dormobile had left Calais, had driven non-stop to Versailles, hoping to catch the advance party on the road.

68

Failing to do so, they had 'swanned around' the square, as Darcy put it, until Jimmy finally spotted the parked Dormobile and recognized the registration number. They touched the radiator of the Dormobile which was still warm and they knew that the others had recently arrived. At first they were uncertain whether they should wait there and be certain of meeting the school party on its return but 'dash it all, the urge for culture', as Darcy said, prevailed and they decided to inspect the place, hoping to bump into the others. There were several 'crocodiles' from English schools touring Versailles that afternoon and Darcy had spoken to several of the mistresses in charge, only to draw a complete blank. He and Jimmy were handicapped because they only knew Jane and Jacky from the party they were looking for—and Jane and Jacky were nowhere to be seen. In the end, they were on the point of returning to the parked Dormobile and waiting there when Jimmy noticed Miss Mark and Valerie standing just inside the Hall of Mirrors. He remembered that Jane had vaguely described their companions and the description, which he was too tactful to give, roughly fitted Miss Mark and Valerie. So Darcy had gone up to them. His joking remark had had disastrous results but Jimmy was now positive that they were on the right trail and so they had followed the fleeing pair. 'And here we are,' Darcy ended, with a flourish of his driving-cap, 'complete with apologies for having scared you.'

The apologies were duly accepted and even the flustered Miss Mark had to admit that she had misread the situation. Then they all walked back to the square and Darcy, quietly prompted by Jacky, prevailed on the rest to permit him to buy them an ice-cream each from the convenient stall nearby. They sat in the sunshine in and around the open Bentley nibbling away at the cones while Darcy spread a road-map across Bertha's high bonnet and discussed plans with Miss Haywood. He had shrewdly guessed that, if he could win her confidence, it would be half the battle in ensuring more freedom for the 'female Jays' once they reached Rome.

While the two school-mistresses were conferring with Darcy, Jimmy had wandereI off with the other two Jays to inspect the Dormobile. Valerie was busy entering up her diary and Margaret sat on the running-board of the old Bentley, gazing vaguely into space and occasionally licking her oozy cornet.

Jane showed him how the bunks pulled down and how the canvas slot in the roof could be raised to make room for an extra pair of bunks. 'Jolly neat,' he said in a faintly wistful tone. 'But, I say, there are only four bunks—and there are six of you. What happens to the other two?'

'Oh, we thought of that,' she said proudly. 'We've got two camp-beds stowed away with the luggage. The idea is we put up a kind of lean-to tent against the side of the bus at night and two of us take it in turns to sleep out there.'

'What about food and cooking?' he asked.

'There's a Calor gas stove in the back of the Dormo,' Jacky told him, 'and a tank of fresh water, too. The old Haybag has worked it out that we'll all have a French breakfast, coffee or tea and croissants, that kind of thing —which won't take any trouble to prepare. For lunch, like today, we have bread and jam or cheese and fruit. Then in the evenings we'll have a proper meal cooked on the stove.'

'Sounds fun,' he said, a shade enviously. 'I just hope you don't run out of gas on the trip. I'd hate to think of you starving out here in the cold while Darcy and I toy with caviare and roast pheasant in some swish hotel!'

'We shan't run out of gas,' his sister said. 'Not so long as Jacky's in the party!'

Jacky was about to retaliate when she caught Miss

Haywood's eye. 'Are you ready now, girls?' Miss Haywood called. 'I think we ought to be moving on.'

Margaret suddenly sat bolt upright. For once her dreamy features were alert. 'Oh, we mustn't go just yet,' she said. 'I haven't taken any pictures.' She began to forage in a big leather bag she carried and pulled out a Leica camera and various bits of equipment, including different sets of lenses and a light meter. She held the latter on her palm and squinted at it. Then she began to fiddle with setting knobs on the camera. She slung the leather strap of the camera round her neck and peered through the view-finder. She unscrewed the lens and screwed in a long-range set. Then she raised the camera to her eyes once more and gazed for a long time. At last, apparently satisfied, she began to prowl to and fro, stopping here and there to decide which was the best angle for a shot of the palace on the hill.

'Well, I must say this is most thoughtless of you, Margaret,' said the vexed Miss Haywood. 'You had all this time for taking photographs and you just sat there doing nothing. Now, just as the rest of us are ready to move on, you have to hold us up in this way. It really is too bad!'

Margaret took not the slightest notice of her. Absorbed in her hobby, she clicked the shutter, wound on the film and then repeated the whole process. She even squatted to get a fancy shot of the palace, silhouetted behind the high bonnet of the Bentley, squeezing her way between the two indignant school-mistresses without the hint of an apology. At last she was satisfied and she slowly put away her precious camera and equipment in the big leather case. She was surprised to find that everyone else had taken their places in the Dormobile, the engine was running and Miss Haywood was about to let in the clutch. Darcy and Jimmy had climbed into the Bentley.

'All aboard!' Jimmy shouted to the dazed-looking girl.

71

'You'd better step on it. It's a goodish walk to Chartres and the last bus is about to leave.'

She gazed at him through her thick glasses, sniffed and then ambled over to the step of the Dormobile, climbed in and sat down next to Valerie, all without a word.

'Boy, they do get some ripe ones at that school,' Jimmy yelled to Darcy above the booming exhaust-note of the car. 'I used to think Jacky and Jane were odd but they're positively normal compared to her!'

*   *   *

For the next two and a half days the cavalcade of two vehicles wound its way across France, pausing awhile to admire the radiant rose-window of Chartres cathedral, the ancient splendour of Orleans and the brooding magnificence of Bourges. Jacky told Jane privately that she had been infected by 'cathedral-itis', a permanent crick in the neck from staring up at the buttresses and shadowy pillars that support the roofs of each of these noble buildings. But secretly all of them realized that they were having a unique opportunity to study the loving care with which whole generations of craftsmen and fashioned symphonies in stone in praise of their Creator. As Miss Haywood pointed out to them, each cathedral was an act of faith in an age when life could be hard and short and dangerous. Even Margaret seemed to absorb her words and went so far as to take her inevitable snapshots at the beginning of each stop and not just as everyone else was waiting to move on.

Early on in their travels, Miss Haywood and Darcy agreed that, as the Bentley could and did go much faster than the Dormobile, it was pointless for them to travel in convoy along the roads of France. At the start of each day they would work out the places of interest to be visited and where they would stop that night, depending

72

on whether or not a good camping site was available.
Then each vehicle would get there separately. Darcy would
usually give the Dormobile a good half-hour's start before he settled his and Jimmy's hotel bill and then he
would take the same route. Sometimes he would overtake
the Dormobile fifty miles away, sometimes he might catch
up only several minutes after it had paused to look at a
château or yet another cathedral. Once he had to stop
and adjust a plug lead that had come adrift and on this
occasion he only caught up with the others as they were
pulling in to their camping place for the night.

Jimmy usually felt a twinge of envy whenever he and
Darcy wished the 'females' good night and went off to find
themselves a comfortable hotel bedroom. He enjoyed
Darcy's company and the thrill of driving fast down the
poplar-lined straight roads in an open car, but the thought
of camping out attracted him. He felt that he was missing
something when he saw the women-folk putting up the
lean-to tent and unpacking the camp-beds or bustling
round preparing the supper on the Calor gas stove. It
seemed all wrong to him that the weaker sex should be
having the fun and excitement of living rough while he
and Darcy relied on hotel service and French *cuisine*.

The 'Dormocade', as Darcy had nicknamed it by con-
tracting the two words 'Dormobile' and 'cavalcade', moved south-east through Lyons, which had solved its traffic
problems by building a car-tunnel underneath the city and
the River Rhône, towards the Italian border. They spent
the night near Grenoble and then, for the first time on
the journey decided to part company for a day or two.
There was no row or major difference of opinion about
the decision. Miss Haywood had read a book about the
passes from France into Italy and she understood that
one of the easiest and least twisty was the Mount Cenis
pass, leading eventually to Turin. Darcy had already
driven along it a couple of times and he assured her that

73

it was a beautifully constructed road with a good many bends but none to cause any trouble as long as it was taken carefully. The road, he told her, also ran straight along a high plateau in the middle of the pass so that, once you had climbed to the top, you had several miles' break from the curves and bends before you had to start descending on the Italian side.

Darcy himself, enthusiastically backed up by Jimmy, wanted to try a more diffcult route into Italy—and one that would be new to him. He decided on the Col de Larche. It was shown on the Michelin map as a thin cork-screwing grey line: the caption on page 1 of the map, explaining what this symbol stood for, read, '*Route accidentée: parcours avec nombreuses déclivités*'.

'Gosh,' said Jimmy, when Darcy showed it to him and Jane, 'that sounds exciting. What does it mean?'

Darcy looked puzzled for a moment and then he improvised. 'A route full of accidents. Some thing or other with numerous declinings.'

Jimmy peered over his shoulder at the map. '*Parcours,*' he muttered. 'It doesn't make sense to me. Isn't French a soppy language, really?'

Valerie, the scholar, happened to overhear them. 'Can I help you?' she asked smugly. 'What is it you don't understand? Oh, the word *parcours*. That's simple. It comes from the verb *parcourir* meaning to travel over. A secondary meaning is "to peruse"—in other words, let your eyes travel over the pages of a book. It's perfectly easy if you take the trouble to study a language, in particular the irregular verbs.' She wandered off with her nose a few degrees higher in the air.

'I can't think how the rest of you stand her all day long,' was Jimmy's observation.

'Anyway, I bet she's wrong,' Jane said, 'because Pat says that *erreur de parcours* in show jumping is French

74

for "wrong course"—f'r instance, taking the wrong jump and getting eliminated.'

'That's what your friend Valerie needs,' Jimmy said savagely. 'To get illuminated, I mean.'

'You mean "eliminated", do you not, young man?' Jane said, imitating her friend's precise tone.

'Eliminated or illuminated—what's the difference?' Jimmy replied. 'Id like to see her name in lights—outside the Chamber of Horrors at Madame Tussaud's! '

'Well, what do you say, Jim m'boy?' Darcy butted in. 'Shall we have a dice with old Bertha on the *route accidentée?*'

'Suits me fine,' Jimmy replied.

And so it was agreed. The Dormobile would try the Mont Cenis pass and then go on through Turin and Alessandria, hitting the Italian coast at Genoa. The Bentley would take the Col de Larche farther south and then drive on to Cunco, dropping to the coast at Savona and then running along by the sea to link up with the other route at Genoa.

Darcy and Miss Haywood felt that they could not be certain of finding each other in such a big city as Genoa, so they decided to drive on independently down the coast another hundred miles or so until they reached Pisa, which should be during the afternoon of the following day. Whichever of the two vehicles arrived there first would wait for the other for the rest of the afternoon and, if necessary, until ten o'clock in the morning of the day after. Barring accidents, it seemed certain that they would be able to join forces within that ample time-limit.

So, on the outskirts of Grenoble, the Dormocade split up. The 'Dormo' part turned away northwards to meet Route N.6 near Chambéry. Darcy and Jimmy in the old Bentley waited and waved until the square-looking van was a speck in the distance. Then they swung southwards in the direction of Gap.

75

The Dormobile party had an uneventful journey. Their route lay along the valley of the River Isère and they made good progress for the first seventy-five miles. Jane and Jacky were quieter than usual and each was privately disturbed at the thought of parting with the Bentley, if only for a day and a half. Valerie had her nose in a guide-book and Margaret sat dreamily gazing at the distant mountains. Miss Haywood was mapreading and Miss Mark kept the Dormobile chugging along cautiously towards the frontier. And so it was a silent group that drove along the valley road, which became twisty and bumpy as they approached Lanslebourg.

Then they started to climb the pine-covered mountainside The road cork-screwed upwards and the Dormobile ground along it in second or third gear. Up it went, always climbing, until it reached the plateau that Darcy had mentioned. This was an eerie place, cold and lonely with patches of mountain mist creeping across the green pastures. Bells tied to the necks of the grazing cattle tinkled forlornly in the distance. Once they drove alongside a broad lake with the peaks of the mountains mirrored on its surface. They were glad to start the descent and see human beings again, first at the French and then at the Italian Customs posts. Here Miss Haywood changed their money into lire and bought a ration of tourists' petrol coupons. They were at last on Italian soil.

They camped for the night not far from Allessandria and were away early next morning. The *autostrada* to Genoa was a great disappointment to Jane and Jacky. They had expected a broad, sweeping motor-road where they had hoped that even their cautious drivers might open up the speed. Instead they found a narrow, winding road that was clogged with petrol-tankers and huge lorries with articulated trailers. The Dormobile only averaged twenty miles an hour on the *autostrada* and the whole party thought it a swindle that they should have to pay a toll of two hundred lire for the privilege of using such a congested highway.

On through the bustling streets of Genoa they drove, past the harbour and out on to the coastroad that jinked and twisted around the headlands above the blue Mediterranean, linking holiday places they had read about like Santa Margherita, Portofino and Rapallo. If Rome had not been the distant goal, the Jays would have been tempted to suggest that they had gone far enough. The sea looked so inviting and the gaudy beach umbrellas so gay. But they sighed and kept their thoughts to themselves. The Olympic Games were only a week or so away and not to be missed at all costs.

At last they were clear of the mountains that swept down almost sheer to the sea and then they were in the long flat plain that leads to Pisa and on, always low-lying and flat, to Rome itself. The Dormobile was still several miles away from the ancient city of Pisa when Jacky spotted the famous Leaning Tower standing out from a huddle of buildings. She nudged Jane and called out to the others. Miss Haywood, who was driving, slowed up and pulled in to the side of the road.

She peered out of the windscreen and then said, 'Well done, Jacqueline—you really have a pair of sharp eyes. Yes, that's the Leaning Tower, all right'

'Was there an earthquake or something to push it over like that?' Jane asked her.

'I'm not sure,' she replied. 'Does anyone here know the answer?'

Valerie drew a deep breath and Jacky muttered, 'Hold tight—make way for the girl wonder.' Valerie glared at her and then said, 'Yes, Miss Haywood, I happen to have looked it up.'

'You would,' Jane said.

'Please, Jane,' Miss Haywood cut in quickly. 'If Valerie

knows the answer, let her speak without interruption. **Go on, Valerie, please.'**

Needing little encouragement, Valerie went on in a sing-song recital. 'The Leaning Tower was intended as a bell tower for the cathedral and is sometimes known as the campanile, which is derived from the Latin word meaning a place for bells. It was begun in A.D. 1173 and finished in 1350. The foundations were laid in sandy soil and when the first three stories were built, the tower began to tip over. The building was continued but the plans had to be modified. The tower is one hundred and eighty feet tall and consists of eight stories built of white marble. If you dropped a stone from the top, it would land on the ground over sixteen feet away from the base.'

'Not necessarily,' Jacky interrupted.

'What do you mean?' Valerie asked indignantly. 'Of course it would. It says so in my book.'

'Well, your book must be wrong then.'

'Of course it's not wrong!'

'Now then, girls, don't let's argue about it If Valerie's book says that a stone would hit the ground sixteen feet from the base, it must be so, Jacqueline. After all, you've never been closer than this to the Leaning Tower, have you?'

'No, Miss Haywood, I certainly haven't. All I'm wondering is—what would happen if you stood on the side of the tower away from the leaning side, if you know what I mean. If you dropped a stone over from that side, it would land on the tower itself, wouldn't it? I mean, it stands to reason, I would have thought.' Jacky looked the picture of earnest innocence.

Jane took her cue. 'I think it's terribly careless of people like the one who wrote Valerie's book going round chucking stones off the top of tall buildings. They might easily kill someone. I'm not sure I want to inspect the

78

tower if there are going to be stones flying around in all directions.'

'And there might not just be stones, either,' Jacky said, neatly catching the conversational ball. 'I don't like the sound of that person who wrote Val's book. He probably flings bricks and lumps of old iron off the top of the tower. I vote we drive straight on and give a dangerous place like that a miss.'

Miss Haywood clapped her hands impatiently. 'Now then, you two, a joke's a joke but this has gone too far. Is there anything more you'd like to tell us about the Leaning Tower, Valerie?'

But Valerie had been put off by the chaffing methods of the two Jays. In a sulky voice she replied, 'No, thank you, Miss Haywood. I don't think the information would be appreciated.'

They drove on into Pisa and inspected the tower and the cathedral itself, fortunately without being hit by any flying objects descending from above. Miss Haywood had arranged to meet Darcy and Jimmy in the piazza near the cathedral and had half-expected to find them waiting for, although the Bentley had not actually passed the Dormobile on the road, it could have easily reached Genoa beforehand and have been in front from then on. But there was no sign of the easily recognizable old car anywhere near the piazza. And so the party decided to sit down at a pavement café, where the girls tucked into cakes and Coca-Cola while the two mistresses drank cups of the espresso coffee. They sat there for over half an hour, continually scanning the square, but Bertha the Bentley never appeared.

It was getting on for six o'clock and another half-hour had gone by while Margaret, having suddenly decided that she ought to photograph the tower and the cathedral, had prowled to and fro, adjusting her camera and taking an infinite time to select the right angle for each shot. Miss

79

Haywood was getting worried but she tried to conceal her anxiety from the younger members of the party. She remembered the twisty, grey lines on the map and Darcy's joking remarks about trying out the *route accidentée*. She knew him to be a capable driver but she privately thought he drove too fast at times. And what if the brakes had failed on the old car? In her mind's eye she could see the smoking debris at the bottom of some steep gulley and the limp bodies of the two occupants stretched out alongside. Catching Miss Mark's eye, she muttered some excuse to the girls and drew her colleague away on the pretext of studying the architecture on the west front of the cathedral. Valerie volunteered to accompany them and for once Miss Haywood was irritated by her zeal for learning. Somewhat snappily, she suggested that Valerie should be in charge of the others until she and Miss Mark returned in a few moments.

'I'm worried, Sheila,' she said, when they were out of earshot. 'Do you think anything can have happened to Flight Lieutenant de Vere and that nice young boy Jimmy?'

'Oh, I'm sure they're all right,' Miss Mark replied with an assumed heartiness. 'Perhaps they've had a puncture— or even lost their way somewhere.'

That's hardly likely—losing their way, I mean. Mr. de Vere seems very capable at map-reading and finding his way about.'

'But they could easily have had a puncture or something wrong with the engine. After all, it's not a new car and, although it's been a very good one in its time, things can go wrong. And there wouldn't be any garage near the frontier.'

Miss Haywood said doubtfully, 'I hope you're right.'

'Another thought has just struck me. They may have got tired of all this sight-seeing and have deliberately taken their time getting here. I can't say that either of them has been really keen to study all the old classical buildings we've seen—though they've been too polite to say so. Perhaps they stopped for a swim at one of those holiday places we passed, like Rapallo or Lerici. I'd say that was more in their line somehow.'

Miss Haywood looked relieved. 'It's quite a tonic to hear your views, Sheila. After all, we did say we'd wait here until ten o'clock tomorrow morning. That gives them plenty of time to catch us up in. Let's get back to the girls, shall we? Valerie's been in charge long enough.'

The setting sun was already casting long shadows across the piazza when they rejoined the others at the pavement café. They climbed back into the Dormobile and drove a few miles to their pre-arranged campng spot by the coast near Marna di Pisa. Supper-time came and went and still there was no sign of Darcy or Jimmy, but Miss Haywood was no longer alarmed at their absence. When Jacky began wondering aloud where they might have got to, she just repeated Miss Mark's arguments, which seemed to satisfy the junior members of the party.

But next morning, after they had dressed and breakfasted, her fears began to return. It was gone nine o'clock and the Bentley had not turned up. Their camp-site was only a few yards from the sea and she gave way to the Jays' repeated pleading for a swim before they drove on. The sun was bright and there was barely a ripple on the placid Mediterranean, so the others went for a dip with Miss Mark in charge while she sat and waited, in case Darcy and Jimmy appeared. She could hear the girls laughing and shrieking as they splashed around in the shallows and even the sedate Valerie caught the spirit of the occasion by swimming under water and tickling Miss Mark's feet. But Miss Haywood was in no mood for sharing their mirth. By this time she was convinced that something had gone wrong.

It was close on ten when the bathe was over and the

81

girls had changed back into their travelling clothes. Indeed it was ten minutes past the hour before the lean-to tent had been folded and stowed away and the camp-site tidied up. Everyone was restless and ill at ease.

'Why are we wasting time?' Valerie asked. 'I vote we drive on.'

'And I vote we hang on here for a bit,' Jacky said bluntly. 'I'm worried about Jimmy and Darcy. What do you think is keeping them, Miss Haywood?'

'Oh, they're bound to be along soon,' came the reply. 'Miss Mark and I suspect they stayed for the night farther up the coast—in one of those attractive little places we passed through yesterday. They probably got tired of all this sight-seeing and decided to stop somewhere for a swim.'

'But a swim doesn't take the best part of a day,' Jane argued. 'They ought to have caught up long ago.'

'Well, they haven't,' Valerie butted in, 'and I think we're just wasting time hanging around here. We'll never get to Rome at this rate.'

'You can keep your old Rome,' Jane retorted 'I just want to know what's happened to our friends.'

'I'm rather afraid Valerie's right,' Miss Haywood said, 'although I wouldn't put it quite so crudely. There's not really much point in our staying here. If they have been held up, they'd probably drive straight through Pisa without stopping and they could be miles ahead of us by now. I think we ought to be moving along. It's over two hundred miles to Rome and we ought to get there and settle in well before dark.'

'But what if they've had an accident?' Jacky asked in concern.

'Frankly, Jacqueline,' Miss Mark said, 'there wouldn't be much we could do. Although, mind you, I'm quite sure they're all right. But if, for the sake of argument, they have had a minor mishap, it could be anywhere between here and Grenoble back in France. And they're both very resourceful. They would either have carried out the repairs themselves of got in touch with a garage somewhere. We couldn't do any good by driving back along the route we think they've taken.'

'I think we'll bump into them along the road—or even find they've reached Rome ahead of us,' Miss Haywood said with assumed heartiness. 'Come along, we'd better start. Somewhere along the road there'll be a loud roar and the Bentley will go racing past us. You mark my words!'

But she was wrong. The Dormobile drove sedately south towards the Eternal City but there was no welcome roar from behind. Nor was there any sign in the driving mirror of a high-winged bonnet coming up fast from the rear. In fact, Bertha the Bentley never reached Rome at all.

CHAPTER FIVE

OVER THE EDGE

IT is the story-teller's privilege to jump backwards and forwards in time, so let us turn back the clock two days—to the moment when Darcy and Jimmy, after watching the Dormobile dwindle in the distance up the long straight road to Chambéry, climbed into Bertha and began to head south. The sun was already blazing down out of a cloudless sky and they welcomed the breeze of the car's motion as they roared towards Gap. Somehow they both felt gay and carefree, like playing truant from school. They had grown to like and respect the two schoolmistresses since first meeting them at Versailles but it was good to be on their own again, away from the restraining influence of culture and sight-seeing. Darcy began to sing aloud 'What Shall We Do With The Drunken Sailor?' and Jimmy joined in the choruses of 'Earl-y in the Morning' in his piercing half-broken treble. They overtook a French peasant plodding along in a farm cart drawn by a patient old horse. 'Bon Jaw. Quelle jolly cheval,' shouted Darcy. The man stared after them suspiciously. He couldn't see what there was to shout about—but then everyone knew that *les Anglais* were a nation of madmen.

Bertha made good progress, although the road began to indulge in *'nombreuses déclivités'* when it crossed the Col Bayard near Gap. From then on it was fairly straight, even when Darcy forked left at Tallard and began to drive east twards the Italian frontier. By noon they had reached Barcillonnette and decided to stop for a picnic lunch. The road ran through a deep valley alongside a turbulent stream. Even in summer it was racing over the boulders in its bed and, judging from the streaks of mud plastered high up on the walls of the houses in the small town, Darcy and Jimmy guessed that in the spring, when it would have been swollen with the extra volume of water from the melting snow on the mountain-side, it must have poured over its banks and flooded the place. For long stretches the tarmac surface had been washed away from the road and the Bentley had to bump slowly over the now muddy, now dusty track.

After their brief halt they started up again, climbing the steep mountain-side above the river valley. A wire had been stretched across the valley and Jimmy watched with awe as a huge tree trunk was hauled from one side to the other on a pulley by the lumberjacks who were cutting down a section of the pine-covered slope on the far side. Darcy was too busy keeping his eyes on the bends and curves of the road to follow Jimmy's gaze.

'I wonder how on earth they get the wire right up there,' Jimmy pondered. 'You'd almost need to trail it along behind an aeroplane.'

Darcy snatched a quick glance at the wire. 'There's only one way to do it,' he said. 'They must attach it to a pole at one end, trail it across the river and up the mountain to the far side, fix it to a pole there and then windlass it in until it's stretched tight across the valley. Simple when you know how!'

'Gosh, Darcy, I think you're wonderful,' Jimmy said in mock admiration. 'Now can you tell me how they put those glass balls in the top of old-fashioned lemonade bottles?'

Darcy grinned at him and then concentrated again on his driving. The road was climbing all the time and there were lots of loose stones on its chalky, dusty surface.

The Bentley was skidding slightly and lurching at each sharp bend and it took all Darcy's attention and judgment to keep it on course. There was a nip in the air and patches of mountain mist rolled suggishly across their path. They were already five thousand feet above sea-level as they approached the French Customs post and had to climb another thousand feet before they reached the top of the pass.

Darcy stopped the car outside the wooden hut that sheltered the two men in blue uniforms from the Gendarmerie Nationale, whose lonely task it was to guard the frontier. One of them stamped his and Jimmy's passports and the other then walked outside, swung up the post that barred their path and wished the travellers 'Bon voyage' as the Bentley roared on.

It took only a few minutes to cross the No-Man's-Land between the French and Italian Customs posts. Again they had to stop for their passports to be examined and stamped and for Darcy to buy his tourist's ration of petrol coupons. The Italians are, man and boy, a nation of car-fanciers: the officials at the frontier clustered round Bertha, gazing with curiosity and admiration at her long bonnet and the proud sweep of her mudguards. One of them murmured 'Bella' bella' and Jimmy, sitting in the passenger seat, was glad to be a small part of the spectacle. The rumble from the exhaust when Darcy started the engine caused further admiring nods from the audience and, as they drew away under the uplifted barrier across the road, Jimmy again felt like royalty making a state visit!

So far, since leaving Barcillonnette, they had been almost alone on the winding, climbing road into Italy. They had met a local bus on the outskirts of the little town and had overtaken a ponderous lorry on its way up to the lumber camp but they had seen no trace of tourists

86

like themselves or private cars. Jimmy yelled above the roar of the engine, 'Pretty lonely road, isn't it?'

'Dash it all, I like it that way,' Darcy shouted back. 'It's too narrow and bendy for a lot of traffic. Just as long as the brakes don't conk out, we're doing fine!'

He had good reason to be concerned about the brakes. Their route was descending all the time now, jinking and bending down towards the lush, green rice-fields of the Po Valley. Bertha's great weight was acting like a second accelerator on the downhill course and Darcy had to keep changing to a lower gear so that the revolutions of the engine would work as an extra brake on their speed. The big car lurched at each corner and Darcy had to grip the wheel with all his strength to hold it on course.

Jimmy had spoken too soon about the lack of other traffic. Suddenly there was the shriek of a high-pitched engine behind them and the arrogant blare of a hooter. Darcy edged the Bentley to the right so that the nearside wheels bumped on the verge, only a few feet from a sheer drop off the mountain-side. A scarlet Alfa-Romeo Sprint Veloce screamed past, the driver grinning and raising a thumb to acknowledge Darcy's courtesy. The Alfa tore up to the next corner, braked violently and, with a plume of dust rising from the spinning rear wheels, slid out of sight. They could hear the rise and fall of the high-pitched engine as it raced on down the valley.

Hardly had the Alfa-Romeo disappeared when there was another imperious hooter-blast from behind them. This time it was a squat, sleek Mercédès gun-metal grey in colour underneath the streaks of mud and dust that spattered its smooth sides. The road happened to cork-screw even worse than usual at this spot and was also too narrow to allow two cars to pass in comfort. The Mercédès was snapping at the heels of the Bentley and the driver kept his hand down on the hooter-button all the time.

'Oh, dry up!' Jimmy muttered. 'What does he expect us to do?—take off and hover overhead while he goes by?'

They came to a short stretch of straight road and Darcy drew over. The Mercédès tore past a fountain of small stones spraying up from its rear wheels. The driver scowled and made no sign of thanks. He braked hard and drifted round the corner, then was off in hot pursuit of the red Alfa. On the next bend Darcy and Jimmy could see a long stretch of the mountain-side. The Alfa was already half a mile ahead, ripping its way up a brief ascent. They could faintly hear the top note of the engine across the quiet valley and then the deeper hum of the Mercédès, which was swiftly catching the little red car, drowned it.

For a moment Darcy thought secretly of joining in the private race but then he shook his head and grinned. He would never have admitted it aloud but he knew that the old Bentley was no match on the mountain road for these modern fast cars. On the straight he might have held the Merc and would probably beat the Alfa but in the thirty years that had passed since the 'Bentley Boys' had dominated the racing world, engines had become lighter and more efficient and brakes and suspension had improved. He was not going to risk Jimmy's life in an unequal contest along a road he didn't know—and a road that contained more curves to the mile than almost any other in Europe!

Alone again on their stretch of unmetalled surface, Darcy and Jimmy motored on. There were patches of green now on the bare, craggy mountain and, dotted here and there, they could see a cottage or a shepherd's hut. Apart from an occasional switchback, the road was descending all the time and soon they would be down in the plain. But, as if in a burst of petulant anger because it was so soon to lose the travellers from its twisted grip, the mountain road bent and wriggled in one long last series of blind corners and hairpin bends. It had been carved out of the side of the cliff and it followed the swerving contour of the mountain-side. To the left, as the Bentley descended, was a sheer wall of rock. To the right, the cliff fell away, plunging down to the valley below. Boulders placed at about five-yard intervals formed a rough barrier between the edge of the road—and nothing.

There was just enough room for two cars to pass—if both were driven carefully and each kept over to its proper side. Darcy fell into the Italian habit of sounding the horn in a sustained blast every time he approached a blind corner. The sound of the Bentley's roaring engine was flung back in a continuous echo off the wall of rock to the left and it was impossible to hear the warning noise of another car coming in the opposite direction. So on every corner Darcy kept as far over to his own side of the road as he dared and Jimmy, watching the marker stones flickering by, wondered if the Bentley's nearside wheels might not scrape along one, so close did they go.

And then it happened As they reached the next right-angle bend, a rush of noise blasted them and a scarlet blur shot into view, charging straight at them. It was the Alfa-Romeo, coming back up the mountain and swinging wide at the corner, head on into the Bentley. Darcy's speed of reaction, the split-second reflexes of the test pilot, saved them. He stabbed at the brake pedal and yanked the wheel in a convulsive heave to the right. Bertha's nose swung across the line of the racing Alfa, missing it by inches. Her front wheel jarred against a marker stone and she swerved farther to the right, scraping the edge of the cliff. She lurched as one wheel plunged over, teetered for a fraction—and then rolled off the road. Darcy ducked and pulled Jimmy down below the level of the bonnet. The big car smashed into a boulder on the cliff and rolled again.

To Jimmy everything seemed to be happening in slow
89

motion. It was like watching an exciting film that suddenly stopped dead. He couldn't imagine that this was actually happening to him Then the Bentley's tumbling progress was finally halted. It crashed into a tree stump, twenty feet below the lip of the road. The jarring impact shot Jimmy's head forward, in spite of Darcy's protecting arm around his shoulders His forehead bashed against the dashboard. There was thunder inside his temples and a lightning flash of blinding light. That was the last he knew before he passed out.

When he came round, he was sitting up on the edge of the road with his back against a marker stone. 'What happened?' he asked and his voice sounded thin and far away as he listened to it. 'What am I doing sitting here?'

Darcy was standing over him, white-faced. 'Thank God you've come round, Jim,' he said hoarsely. 'Dash it all, I thought you were a goner, lying there and hardly breathing. How do you feel?'

'A bit dazed,' Jimmy answered. 'Ow!' he added in anguish as he moved his head.

'Not surprising,' Darcy said, 'You've got a lump on your noggin the size of an egg!'

'But what *happened*?' Jimmy asked again.

'We ran out of road—at least, we were forced off the road. If I ever lay eyes on that cretin in the Alfa, I'll wring his blinking neck! He came charging round the corner so wide that I either had to hit him head-on or swerve away. And you see what happened in swerving!' He pointed dramatically down the slope. As Jimmy peered over, the movement made his head swim. Blinking to clear his vision, he saw the pathetic sight of Bertha lying on her side half-way down, like some pre-historic monster that was mortally wounded. One wheel was still revolving slowly, a dying reflex.

'Oh, Darcy,' he said in anguish and tears stung at his eyes. 'What are we going to do?'

'You sit there for the moment. I'll flag down the first car that comes this way and see if we can beg a lift into —whatever the name of the next town is. Then we'll get a doctor to have a look at your head. Thank Heavens it's a hard one!' and Darcy gave a ghost of his old grin. 'But I want to be sure you haven't got concussion or anything. Then I'll have to arrange for a breakdown truck to come out and winch poor old Bertha back on the road . . .'

'Will she be all right?' Jimmy cut in anxiously.

'. . . Hard to say. I had a quick look-see while you were still out. She's had an awful bashing on the side that took all the impact. I reckon the front wheel's a write-off and the suspension that side has probably gone. The I-ties are marvellous engineers but the problem's going to be getting spare parts. There aren't all that number of thirty-year-old Bentleys knocking round Northern Italy! Oh, I could murder that Alfa driver!'

'So that's the end of our holiday in Rome?'

''Fraid so, Jimmy, m'boy. It'll take at least a week to get Bertha going again—that is, if she ever can be made roadworthy. And the cost of repairs will clear me out of travellers cheques. The only consolation is that we both came out of it all right. The pair of us could easily have been killed!'

'Are you okay, Darcy? I ought to have asked you sooner.'

'Me? I'm fine.'

Jimmy saw that Darcy was surreptitiously tying a handkerchief round his right wrist by holding one end in his teeth. 'But what about your wrist?' he asked.

'That's nothing much. Just a graze I got when we hit that tree-stump. Lucky we did. The next stop would have been the bottom—and that would have seen us both off. Jim, I can hear a car coming! I'll nip round the corner and stop him.'

91

Left alone, Jimmy supported his aching head in his hands. He had never felt more wretched. As Darcy had said, it was something to have come out of the accident alive but at that moment he would just as soon be dead. Bertha may be written off for good, no Rome, no holiday —all because some selfish pig of a driver couldn't keep to his right side when taking a corner. In the background, Jimmy heard a car pull up and then he could distinguish Darcy's voice and another lighter foreign replying. But he felt too dejected to look round. It seemed that Darcy at first sounded indignant and the other voice was quick and apologetic. Then he heard Darcy chuckle and somehow a weight was lifted off his gloomy mind. Footsteps sounded close behind him.

'Jim, we've landed on our feet!' Darcy said. 'This is the character in the Alfa who forced us off the road. He had to drive on and find a spot wide enough to turn round in and now he's coming rushing back to help. He's full of apologies—as far as I can understand him—and admits it was all his fault.

Jimmy's grumbling comment was, 'That's splendid—but I don't see how it's going to get old Bertha back on the road.'

'Ah, that's where the luck comes in. Signor Alfieri— he's just handed me his card, that's how I know his name —well, he's father runs a big garage outside the next town. He's going to run us in and fix up a breakdown truck for Bertha.'

Jimmy looked up. The young Italian stood alongside Darcy. His woebegone features and contrite air clashed with his gaily coloured T-shirt. He burst into a flood of broken English when Jimmy caught his eye. He told them both several times just how sorry he was to have caused the accident and how he praised God that they had not been killed. 'Me—it is all-a my *culpa*,' he added. 'I must set it right. I will pay-a for all things to correct the *auto* again. It will be—how you say?—on the home.'

'He means "on the house", doesn't he?' Jimmy asked.

'*Si, si*,' the young man went on. 'The English idiom—ver' difficult. My English—no good.'

'A sight better than my *Italiano*,' Darcy said. He and the young Italian scrambled down the slope and removed the personal belongings from the battered Bentley. Back on the road again, they helped Jimmy, who still felt muzzy and weak-kneed, into the back seat of the low-slung Alfa. Darcy slid his long legs into the front passenger seat and Signor Alfieri got behind the left-hand drive steering-wheel. The red car tore off down the mountain-side but Darcy noted with an inward smile that the driver took each corner with great care, keeping well to his right side.

'You will rest-a at my house,' said the Italian, 'and when you are feeling fresh as the bluebell . . .'

'Fresh as a daisy,' Jimmy automatically corrected him.

'. . . *Si*, fresh as a daisy, you can drive on this afternoon, if you wish.'

'Drive on in what?' asked Darcy. 'Dash it all, you Italians are great engineers and all that but it'll take more than a couple of hours to get our car going again!'

And then, with a charming white-toothed smile, Signor Alfieri explained his plan. He would lend them the Alfa-Romeo they were driving in for the rest of their holiday. Darcy had told him that they were travelling to Rome—and the car could be theirs as long as they wanted it. He and his father would repair the Bentley, which would be waiting for them when they returned to Northern Italy on their way back to England.

Darcy twisted round in the front seat and stared at Jimmy. Neither of them could grasp at first the artless generosity of the young Italian. Darcy was the first to gather his wits together.

'I can hardly believe it,' he said. 'You're being far too generous.'

'No, no,' replied Signor Alfieri earnestly. 'I see it this-a way. If it had not been for my stupid—how you say? —blunderbuss . . .'

'Blunder,' Jimmy corrected him.

'*Si*, blunder—I should perhaps keep you with me as my English tutor,' he smiled. 'But if it had not been for my folly, you would still be driving along our Italian roads, enjoying yourselves full of peace. It is I, Alfredo Alfieri, who has hurt your *auto* and might have caused your deaths. I am a *cretino*,' he tapped his chest with one gloved hand, 'and I must repair my fault.'

'But how do you know I'll be able to drive this little beauty?' Darcy asked. 'I've never driven one before.'

The Italian answered at once. 'Only a good driver would have avoided a hit up there on the mountain. That tells me all I need to know. You are a good driver.'

'But are you quite sure you can spare the car for two weeks?' Jimmy queried him.

He laughed. 'My father is a *garagista*, as I tell you. He has five, ten cars for me to drive. But for two weeks I will have no time to drive. I shall be busy helping him to correct your fine car!'

And so it was arranged. In spite of all their arguments, Signor Alfieri would not budge. He was determined to make up for his dangerous driving by lending them his Alfa-Romeo for the rest of their holiday.

Darcy even said, 'Look, let's be realistic. You don't know anything about us—we could be a pair of crooks for all you know. How can you be sure we won't just disappear with your car, sell it and then just make off with the proceeds? It must be worth three or four times as much as my old Bentley.'

The young Italian smiled and said, 'If you were a crook, you would not mention that point! My father—he fought with the partisans. He always tell-me, "Alfredo, you can trust the English". Besides, I may be a *cretino* at driving but I think I can tell an honest man. And you are one.'

'I've been called a lot of things in my time,' Darcy retorted, 'but now I'm really blushing!'

The Alfa had reached the outskirts of Cuneo and soon Alfieri swung in into the entrace of a large garage. His father emerged, a portly older edition of the son, and they burst into a torrent of liquid Italian, accompanied by many gestures. At length the father turned to Darcy and Jimmy, shook them both by the hand, bowed and said 'Good night, good night,' in a heavy accent.

'My father no speak English,' Alfredo explained. 'Maybe two words. Please excuse him.' He talked some more Italian and by the way he brought his fist close together and then at the last moment swung one sharply away, they guessed that he was telling his father about the near-accident. Finally, the elder Alfieri nodded his head and flashed his teeth in a warm smile. He waddled away and began to give instructions to a couple of mechanics who were standing nearby watching the pantomime. One of them climbed into a big breakdown truck and began to reverse it into the street.

'They know where to go,' explained the younger Alfieri. 'You must have lunch with us and I will get a *dottore* to examine your head,' he said to Jimmy.

'Oh, it feels fine now.'

'No, I insist. We must be sure here is no injury. It will take two hours, maybe, to bring your car back here. You will need to wait and get your baggages, so you must eat with us and be examined by the *dottore*.'

Darcy and Jimmy, not unwillingly, allowed themselves to be taken into the Alfieri house which adjoined the garage and there met a jolly middle-aged woman, Signora Alfieri, Alfredo's mother. They washed off the dust and grime of their accident and then sat down to an enormous meal of spaghetti and veal, helped down by a flask of Chianti wine in its wicker basket. Alfredo told them that, apart from helping his father in the garage, he also tested fast cars and went in for road-racing. He had driven in the last Mille Miglia and he talked reverently about Stirling Moss and Juan Fangio. Darcy and Jimmy were equal enthusiasts and soon the conversation was bouncing to and fro like a ping-pong ball on the subject of speed. Names like Ferrari, Vanwall, Cooper Climax, B.R.M. and Maserati were batted backwards and forwards. When Jimmy told Alfredo that Darcy was an R.A.F. pilot in a high-speed experimental flight, the latter's eyes opened wide in admiration.

The doctor arrived after lunch, examined the bump on Jimmy's head, flashed a pencil-like torch into both his eyes and then pronounced that he was free from concussion —at least, that was what he and Darcy understood from the medical man's voluble chatter. Jimmy no longer felt dazed and giddy; the lunch and the rest had put him right.

By the middle of the afternoon the breakdown truck returned, towing the battered Bentley which had her nose high in the air as though disdainful of this ignominious way of travelling. The damage was less than Darcy had feared. The stub axle of the offside front wheel would need replacing and the wheel itself was buckled. The body-work on the same side was badly dented and the chassis would need straightening out. The young Alfieri interpreted his father's expert comments and told Darcy that a week's work should see the Bentley 'as right as the snow' —which Jimmy in turn interpreted to mean 'as right as rain'.

They transferred their suitcases into the back of the Alfa-Romeo. A garage hand topped it up with petrol and Alfredo explained the function of the various dials and knobs on the dashboard. Then he went off and came back with an explanatory letter he had written in Italian, just in case a policeman should wonder why two typical English people should be driving round Italy in a typically local car with Italian number plates—and stop them to find out the reason.

By half-past four, more than five hours after Bertha had plunged over the mountain-side, they were ready to go on their way. The Alfieri family gathered to see them off and Signora Alfieri thrust a large basket of fruit and a flask of Chianti into Jimmy's hands. Then, much to his confusion, she gathered him to her ample bosom and kissed him fondly on both cheeks. The men-folk shook hands in turn, then Darcy and Jimmy climbed into the low-slung car. A final wave all round, Darcy gunned the engine and they were off.

At first it was strange to be sitting so close to the ground after their journey in the lofty Bentley, and it took Darcy a mile or two to get used to the lightness of the steering and the nippier acceleration. But soon they had settled back in their seats and had time to talk over their luck. What at at first had seemed a disastrous end to their holiday had turned out to be a splendid new start.

They decided to stop for the night as soon as they reached the coast at Savona. They knew that they were a long way behind the Dormobile but once they got on to the long straight roads from Spezia onwards, they should have little difficulty in catching up. So, after a swim next morning, they drove on through Genoa and down the west coast. The Dormobile had left Pisa before they reached there and, with only a passing glance at the famous Leaning Tower, they pushed on. Just outside Grosseto, a hundred and twenty miles north of Rome, they saw the square-looking van half a mile ahead. Darcy accelerated and the Alfa surged on in pursuit. It slid in behind the Dormobile and Darcy began to play a fanfare on the blaring hooter.

97

D

Back inside the Dormobile, everyone was now terribly worried at the absence of their friends. As the miles slipped past and there was still no sign of the old Bentley. Jane and Jacky were convinced that some terrible accident had happened to it. Miss Haywood had tried to keep a brave face showing but she too was secretly distraught with anxiety. Even Valerie took her nose out of the guidebook to wonder aloud what could be delaying the old car and its male occupants whom she rather despised for their lack of culture. So it was with strained nerves that the Dormobile party listened to the tootling noises coming from immediately to their rear.

'What a bunch of road-hogs some of these Italian drivers are, Jacky remarked bitterly. 'Why doesn't he pull out and overtake us, instead of sitting on our tail and making all that noise?'

Valerie craned round in her seat and gave a withering glance at the Alfa-Romeo. 'There's a horrid boy in the front actually waving at us,' she said. 'What impertinence!'

Jane took a look. 'It may be a horrid boy,' she said quietly. 'In fact, I know he is at times. It's Jimmy!'

The Dormobile nearly swerved off the road as Miss Mark, who was driving, tugged the wheel round at the shock of hearing Jane's last few words. She slowed down and then stopped. The Alfa pulled up right behind and, in a moment, both vehicles emptied and the occupants rushed over to greet each other. Laughing explanations followed and then, much relieved at being united, the convoy drove on sedately towards Rome.

CHAPTER SIX

THE JAYS FOIL A PLOT

ROME was a revelation. They had seen nothing like it before. The casual blend of old and new, the cars and motor-scooters whirled and eddied around the ancient stones of the Colosseum and Hadrians Arch, the soaring white marble of the Piazza Venezia, the broken monuments in the Forum alongside, the cobblestones and the catacombs of the Ancient Appian Way, the splendour of St. Peter's with its immense courtyard, its fountains and its colonnade topped with statues. Rome they discovered, was no carefully preserved museum to the past. It was alive and vigorous, absorbing and recreating the past. It poured out its treasures with a prodigal hand to the passer-by. The Trevi Fountain, a masterpiece of frozen movement with water gushing and trickling down the rocks beneath the pair or rearing horses, was tucked away up a side-alley off the Via del Corso. It was not regarded with silent awe by the Romans as one of the finest groups of statuary in the world. Cars and scooters hooted and ground in low gear in and out of the narrow approaches to it. Touts sold photograph albums, children ran about in play, tourists stood with their backs to the Fountain and threw coins over their left shoulders into the limpid water, following the old superstition that this act would guarantee their return to Rome one day.

Rome, they found over and over again, was like that, a gigantic modern oyster shell that contained many a hidden pearl. You had to climb up a narrow passage-way off a busy street to reach the dark, old Church of Saint Peter in Chains, discreetly sited in a quiet corner of the city. It contained a jewel of sculpture, perhaps the greatest single statue in the world, the statue of Moses carved by Michelangelo. Even Darcy drew in his breath when he saw the huge seated figure which seemed to be pulsating with serene life, so realistic was the flowing beard and every fold of the long gown that was draped casually over the right knee. And under the gleaming altar, set behind a glass panel, was a length of rusty chain, the very same links that had been used by Herod to bind Saint Peter.

It was the same with the Castle of Sant'Angelo. A white-coated policeman directed the rushing traffic on the Victor Emmanuel bridge below its ponderous walls. Inside, you could climb the long, winding passage-way, up and up, marvelling at the dungeons, the collections of weapons, the living quarters of the Popes who used the fort as a sanctuary when Rome was invaded in the sixteenth century. The top of the fort was crowned by a marble angel which had stood there proudly for over two hundred years and from this upper balcony the whole panorama of Rome lay spread out for the spectator to see. And the Romans, being a practical people who consider the needs of the body as well as the mind, high up in the fortifications had set a café which served espresso coffee and delicious cakes!

Rome was more crowded than ever in this Olympic year. All the approaches to the Stadium, which had been constructed on the north-western outskirts of the city, were blocked with hooting traffic. Hotels were overflowing with visitors and even the camping sites were full. The Dormobile party only just managed to squeeze into the huge camp near the E.U.R., the Exhibition centre that had been built on the south edge of the city. Darcy and Jimmy had to go father afield to find a hotel with a room to spare. They ended up at Castel Fusano, nearly twenty miles away on the coast. Luckily, it was linked to Rome by the *autostrada*, a dual carriage-way road that had been built in the days of the dictator Mussolini before the war. Their borrowed Alfa could do the trip in just over twenty minutes and they could even fit in a swim in the sea after breakfast before racing up the tree-lined road to meet the others for a day's sight-seeing.

They had been in Rome for three days when I arrived by air. We had a joyous reunion and it was then that I heard all about their various adventures which have occupied the last two chapters. I fear that my arrival rather spoiled the Jays' concentration on culture!

In previous Olympic Games the show jumping had occupied one day. Each competitor jumped two separate rounds and his total of faults (or his clear rounds if he was exceptionally skilful and fortunate) gave his position both in the individual and in the team championships. Each team consisted of three riders and the team with the lowest total of faults won the gold medal for teams, even though the individual gold medal winner might be a member of another team. Actually, in 1952 although Great Britain won the team gold medal, it was Pierre Jonquères d'Oriola, of France, who won the individual medal in the jump-off, with a South American, Major Oscar Cristi, of Chile, winning the individual silver medal.

This year the show jumping was to have two days to itself. The competition for the individual winner would take place on the seventh of September and the team championships on the eleventh. So it was essential for the horses and riders who were competing in both events to reach a peak of fitness twice in four days and also to key themselves up mentally for two supreme efforts in such a short time.

The day after my arrival, the Three Jays managed to persuade Miss Haywood to let them off sightseeing so that they could watch the team training for the Games. Valerie preferred the sculptured horses of Bernini to their living counterparts and she sniffed when Jacky, somewhat half-heartedly, asked if she would like to go with them. Margaret must have made the fortunes of several Roman shops by the innumerable rolls of film she had bought and used; she also decided that shooting at non-moving targets was more in her line, so the Jays for once were unaccompanied when they reached my hotel. I was, however, surprised to see Darcy tagging along with them. I knew of old just how much he disliked horses.

'What brings you here, Darcy?' I asked.

'Inspecting my investment, Pat.'

'Your investment? I don't understand.'

'It's like this, Pat. The other afternoon, my poor old aching feet couldn't stand another yard of all this marble-bashing up and down the aisles of ancient churches. Dash it all, I'm a flyer, not an infantryman! So when the rest of these eager young beavers decided they just had to notch up yet another church to the five hundred or so they've already seen, I decided to let them get on with it. Saint John Lateran, I think it was—you know, the big one the other side of the Colosseum.'

'I know it,' I said.

'Well, I sat down at one of those pavement cafés in the square and took a little—er—light refreshment. A couple of swarthy types were sitting at the next table arguing the way these I-ties do, you know, waving their fists in each other's faces as though they were about to start a fight, although they're probably the best of friends. Well, I didn't take much notice until one of them mentioned your name and added some figures.'

'Vital statistics, perhaps,' murmured Jimmy, who was listening and who must have been reading a film-fan magazine. I made as if to cuff him and he ducked away.

102

'No,' said Darcy, 'they were odds. These two characters were making a book on the Games. I turned round and spoke to them in my best broken Italian and asked if anyone could join in the jolly fun. They seemed agreeable, so the long and the short of it is I've got five thousand lire on you, Pat. You're a valuable property, m'girl.'

'Darcy, you're crazy,' I said. 'Do you mean to say you handed over five thousand lire—nearly three pounds—to a couple of complete strangers sitting in a café?'

'Sure,' he answered. 'Don't worry, they gave me a receipt. I've got it in my wallet.'

'Of course, they gave you a receipt. Why shouldn't they? But I'm willing to wager there's no address on it and you can't read the signature properly. You might just as well have thrown the money away—or given it to charity.'

'So he did, Pat,' Jacky, who had overheard our discussion, commented. 'The old age pension scheme for broken down crooks!'

Darcy looked abashed and even the tips of his handlebar moustache seemed to droop. 'Dash it all, Pat, I only did it to show my faith in you,' he said. 'These two characters I talked to reckoned that somebody called d'Inzeo—at least, it sounded like two people with the same name—would walk away with the individual gold medal. I wasn't going to let the side down, so I slammed my dough on you for a win.'

'Darcy, you're sweet!' I replied, and now he looked even more embarrassed. 'They were talking about the d'Inzeo brothers, Piero and Raimondo. Both are brilliant riders and either of them could easily win. Incidentally, what odds did you get?'

'Ten to one,' he said. 'Think of it, Pat, fifty thousand lire. We'll have a real party to celebrate the night you win! I'll even invite those weird friends of the Jays—the snooty girl and the one with the camera.

'Hey, slow down, Darcy,' I said. 'Don't let's count any

chickens just yet. This is going to be the climax of four year's training and ambition for all these competitors. The best riders and the best horses in the world are going to be there on the seventh, each one determined to do his best. The slightest error of judgement, the stride that's a few inches too long or two short, the shade too much or too little impulsion—and that could be the end of four years' hopes and efforts. It's not even like an athletic event where the runner only has to rely on himself. In show jumping, the rider can feel a hundred per cent fit and perhaps the horse is a bit off colour or doesn't particularly want to try that day. Or the horse may be in top form and the rider too strung up. No, I've been through it before— at Stockholm—and I wouldn't dare to forecast the results. Besides, if things did just work out right on the big day, you'd still have to catch up with the men who've got your money!'

'Touché, Pat,' he answered with a grin.

Jacky said, 'Do let's get along to the training, please. We've only got today free.'

Somehow the five of us managed to squeeze into the borrowed Alfa-Romeo and I directed Darcy to the area where all the horses were stabled.

Flanagan was just being loaded into the horsebox along with Franco, Hollandia and Sunsalve. I told Paul that I would meet her at Galoppatoio in the Villa Borghese gardens where we were going to work the horses.

Darcy drove us past the Piazza di Siena, where the Grand Prix dressage was being held the next day and where we would be jumping for the Individual competition on Wednesday. While we waited for the horses, we helped put up some fences. Today we were jumping doubles of parallel bars. Meantime the box arrived and Paul brought Flanagan over to me and gave me a leg up. I walked him once round the track of the Galoppatoio to work off any stiffness.

It was pleasant under the trees shading the track but the horse flies were real blood suckers. Flanagan swished his tail so much that it was quite thin by the end of his Roman holiday! I tried to help him by killing any flies that settled but while I killed one another would be biting him. The flies did not bother him while we were cantering and he cheered up, giving a few bucks as he was feeling very fit. He nearly caught me napping when he suddenly shied at the man with the hose who was watering the track to lay the dust.

After about twenty-five minutes I rode Flanagan back to the jumping arena where David Broome had just finished jumping Sunsalve. There were a couple of small fences which I jumped three or four times just to warm him up. Colonel Talbot-Ponsonby walked over to the parallel bars with Bob Armstrong, who was in charge of all our horses. He signalled that he was ready for me to jump that fence. Flanagan was only too keen to get going and each time we jumped, the parallel bars were pulled out wider—the fifth time it was a six-foot spread and Flanagan jumped it freely and well. We then jumped a short course, including a double of parallel bars which we actually met in both the Individual and Team competitions. Flanagan was in tremendous form and indeed he had hardly had a fence down in all his training work. He was sweating a bit when we had finished so Paul took his saddle off and led him round under the trees. We had been lucky to arrive in Rome after the heat wave, so the temperature was not too hot for comfort.

I was going back to the stables in the box when all the horses had finished working, so I went to say Good-bye to Darcy and the Jays. They were still watching in the arena where I joined them.

'Flan was super,' said Jane excitedly. 'Please can we come and watch tomorrow?'

105

'Certainly,' I smiled at her. 'It'll be a bit cooler as we've got a 5 a.m. start tomorrow?'

Complete silence greeted my remark, so I gathered that the enthusiasm for watching us at work only began after normal breakfast time!

'That's why I've seen no worms around; the early birds must have had them all.' Jimmy and Jacky nodded in agreement with Darcy.

'Ah well, leave me to admire the Roman dawn and I'll be seeing you sometime when I can escape from behind the barbed wire of the Villaggio Olimpico. I hope you enjoy yourselves and not so much of that gambling round cafés, please.' The box was ready and I ran over to it, leaving them to watch the Turkish and Roumanian teams who were next on the rota for the use of the training arena.

I saw nothing of the Jays and Darcy for the next couple of days. They were busy rounding off their sight-seeing and I, too, was busy, with the rest of the British team, in the final stages of training for the great occasion.

The tension mounted as the Day came nearer. Even the horses seemed to realize that something special was about to happen. When we came to get them ready for their work, they were alert and excited from their surroundings, snorting and shying at objects that would normally not have attracted any of their attention.

At lunch-time on the Monday, two days before the Individual Championship was to be held, I returned to my hotel after the morning session to find Darcy and Jimmy waiting for me. They both looked anxious.

'What's the matter?' I asked. 'Someone fallen in the Trevi Fountain?'

'It's no joke, Pat,' Darcy said gravely. 'We came rushing round here to see you because we've discovered a plot!'

'A plot,' I echoed. 'Look, Darcy, I've got too much on

my mind to enjoy a leg-pull. This is September the fifth, you know—not the first of April!'

'Honestly, Pat,' he said, 'this is no leg-pull. This is serious. We wouldn't bother you if it weren't, would we, Jim?'

Jimmy shook his head. I realized that they were in earnest. They both liked practical jokes but I knew they would draw the line at making me the victim just before an important competition.

'Tell me all about it,' I said.

'It's like this,' Darcy began. 'You remember you teased me the other day about chucking my money away on that bet. You reckoned I'd never see either of those characters again who took my money and gave me a receipt. Well, I got to thinking about what you said. The sight seeing lark has been dropped this week so yesterday afternoon Jimmy and I thought we'd go back to the café near Saint John Lateran and do a bit of detective work. We sat there for about half an hour, drinking an espresso each, and nary a sign of my two friends. Luckily, there was a waiter there who was a friendly sort of cove and he spoke quite good English. I described the two men to him and he remembered them. He said they didn't seem to do any real work for a living but were always with money.'

'You bet,' I observed. 'Just as long as there are English tourists with five thousand lire to spare!'

'That one was below the belt, Pat,' Darcy replied with a grin. 'Anyway, the waiter told us he didn't know their real names but one was known as Il Lupo and the other Pietro di Bolzano . . .'

'The Wolf and Bolzano Pete—it sounds just like a gangster story,' I butted in.

'. . . That's just what it is.' Darcy went on. 'According to our waiter-chum, they're a pair of thorough crooks with a record as long as your arm. Their main hangout, he said, is over in Trastevere but they often work the cafés

107

near the main tourist centres like Saint Peter's and John Lateran, hoping to find a few mugs to fleece.'

'I hate to say it, Darcy, but it looks as though they've succeeded at least once!'

'Hold on, Pat—not so fast. I gave the waiter a good tip and he told us the restaurant in Trastevere where they usually eat.'

'I wonder why he was so forthcoming with all this information,' I queried. 'Somebody told me the other day that if crooks and confidence-tricksters use a certain café a lot, they usually make it worth the owner's while. Your waiter-friend sounds almost too righteous to be true.',

'The same thought occurred to me, Pat. In fact, I asked him point-blank why he was telling me all this. He said he was saving up to start a café of his own and he thought this pair of crooks were too blatant in the way they skinned tourists. Sooner or later, someone would complain to the police and they would raid the café. He didn't want his name on the police files as a possible accomplice. It might mean that he wouldn't be granted a licence to start a café of his own. So he was all for someone throwing a scare into the Wolf and his chum, Bolzano Pete.'

'That sounds fair enough, Darcy. Tell me more.'

'Well, last night Jimmy and I thought we'd pay a visit to Trastevere and see what else we could find out. I reckoned that people would take less notice if I had a youngster like Jimmy with me, instead of being on my own.'

'That was taking a bit of a risk,' I said rather sharply. 'You're old enough to look after yourself but Jimmy here's only a boy after all. It might have been nasty if trouble had started.'

Jimmy had been silent all this while, listening intently to Darcy's story. Now he went red and butted in with, 'I can look after myself, Pat. We learn judo at school.'

'I know you're tough, Jim,' I said to pacify him, 'and

108

I'm sure you could hold your own in a straight fight. But some of these crooks carry guns or knives—and wouldn't hesitate to use them. Anyway, nothing did happen to you obviously or else you wouldn't be here now. Sorry, Darcy, I keep on interrupting you. I promise to hold my tongue from now on.'

'Thanks, Pat. Well, as I was saying, we drove across the Garibaldi Bridge into the district of Trastevere. I hadn't realized till then that the name means literally "across the Tiber". It's the real old-fashioned part of Rome. narrow little alleyways and dark old houses—quite spooky, in fact. Every now and then it opens out into a small square and there were lots of these open-air restaurants in the squares. Some pretty smart cars, Lancias and Alfas and even a Rolls-Bentley, were parked around the place, too.'

'Trastevere's got very popular,' I observed. It's quite the smart thing for film-stars and celebrities to go and dine there. Oh, Heavens, there I go again interrupting you! Sorry, Darcy—this time really is the last!'

'Your apology is acepted!' he smiled. 'Well, we tooled around in the Alfa until we found the right address. Nobody took any notice of us or the car, whereas if we'd been in poor old Bertha, we'd have stopped the show. We parked the Alfa right alongside the restaurant the waiter had mentioned and, bingo! —not five yards away we saw the Wolf and his chum from Bolzano sitting at a table and deep in conversation with a short, darkish chap. They didn't spot us, luckily. The one called Bolzano Pete did glance up casually but he couldn't see us inside the Alfa and it looked just like any other local make of car to him, I suppose. Anyway, we slid out when they weren't looking and managed to get a table next door. I ought to have mentioned that most of these outdoor cafés and restaurants have lattice-work partitions with greenery growing on them between the tables. I reckon it's supposed

109

to make the place more private and romantic if you happen to be dining out with your girl-friend! We were lucky enough to be sitting right alongside these underworld characters and could hear every word they said without their seeing us.'

'Listen to this next bit carefully, Pat,' Jimmy said eagerly. 'This is the pay-off.'

'Of course I'm listening,' I said. 'This is better than a television thriller! Sorry, Darcy, do go on.'

He leaned forward. 'And, what's more, it happens to be true, too,' he said. 'Well, these three villains had their heads together and were muttering away quietly. It was all Jimmy and I could do to catch the gist of their conversation. In fact, Jimmy couldn't catch it all—*because they were speaking Spanish.*'

'Are you sure, Darcy? I mean, you're no expert at languages, if you don't mind my saying so. I would have thought than any foreign language would sound like Spanish to you!'

'That's just where you're wrong, Pat,' he retorted triumphantly. 'Oh, I know you're thinking of the time I made a mess of French when that gendarme stopped us but what you don't know is that last year we had an officer from the Chilean Air Force attached to my flight. He roomed with me and I learned a lot of Spanish off him. I can't speak the lingo all that well but, dash it all, I can understand what people are saying in it. So there!'

'Do accept my apologies, please,' I said. 'All right, so they were talking in Spanish. What were they saying?'

'This. It seems that the short, dark chap is a groom attached to one of the South American teams taking part in the showing jumping on Wednesday. The other two were in the act of bribing him to drug the more likely horses so that an outsider they fancied might stand a chance of winning!'

At first I could hardly grasp the meaning of Darcy's

last remark. It seemed so fantastic. Jimmy must have spotted my expression for he asked, 'Is it feasible, Pat? Could someone drug the favourites so that they jumped badly on the big day?'

'I honestly don't know, Jimmy. In ordinary horse-racing, trainers are very occasionally warned off for administering drugs to make a horse run faster or slower—that's why the stewards can ask for a saliva test. But for show jumping a horse needs judgment rather than sheer speed. I've never come across a case of an owner or rider giving a horse a pep pill before a big event! On the other hand, if some unscrupulous person wanted to weaken a rival's horse so that it jumped badly, there probably are pills that would slow a horse up or put it off colour. I just don't know.'

'But, supposing there are such drugs,' Darcy asked, 'would it be possible for this South American groom to slip one to each of the likely winners without being spotted?"

I thought hard for several moments. Then, reluctantly, I nodded. 'The whole thing sounds like a bad dream but I suppose it is just about practicable. The horses are all stabled in the same area. There must be nearly a hundred of them, with only about twenty standing a real chance of coming in the first three. Their feed is all stored centrally and the grooms are issued with the ration for each team as required—though I'd have thought it would be terribly difficult to mix drugs into all that amount and be reasonably sure that all the fancied horses would get just enough to put them off colour, but not so much as to rouse the judges' suspicions. The spectators would soon start murmuring if all the best horses just lolloped round the ring, knocking fences down right and left! A criminal who wanted to get away with it quietly would have quite a mob on hand.

'I see that,' Darcy said. 'Let's write off drugging the

feed as being too tricky. But what about the water? Horses have to drink, don't they?'

'My goodness, Darcy,' I said, 'you're on to something there! I never thought about the water supply. Let me think now—I'm trying to remember where the drinking-water comes from. There must be a lot of taps as the water is within easy reach of all the boxes.'

Darcy said, 'I'm no plumber but I reckon each of those taps must lead to a central tank somewhere. It wouldn't be difficult, I imagine, for an expert to work out just how much a hundred horses are likely to drink in any one day. He's then only got to get at the main tank when no one's looking and slip in the right quantity of drugs. Then he just makes sure that the horse he wants to win doesn't drink water from the taps. It's as simple as that!'

The three of us looked at each other in turn. I noticed that Jimmy's eyes were dilated with awe. I expect mine were the same. This was a wide-awake nightmare: I could hardly believe it.

Jimmy broke the silence. 'It seems such a crazy thing to do,' he said. 'Apart from being criminal. I mean, even if he drugged all the favourites, it doesn't follow that his choice is going to win.'

'No,' I replied, 'but it improves the odds enormously—and if those two gangsters did intend to go through with their bookmaking, it would save them paying out a lot of money. Let's just assume that the horse the groom wants to back is a reasonably good one. The Olympic course is bound to be stiff, in fact the toughest course in the world this year. A pretty good horse would probably hit two fences, say, in each of its two rounds—that's a grand total of sixteen faults. In the ordinary way at least a dozen other competitors would do as well as that—or better. But if you could get at the other twelve, give them a drug to slow up their reflexes and make them lose their boldness just for that day, then the moderately good horse

112

would stand a real chance if it kept its usual form.'

'Surely the officials would get suspicious if all the best horses jumped badly on the big day?' Darcy asked.

'There might be safety in numbers,' I answered. 'What I mean is this. If your theory is right about the groom drugging the water-supply, then all the competitors except the one he fancies are going to be off colour—not just the absolute favourites. If someone spotted that only the real favourites did badly, they would almost certainly wonder why. But if ninety-nine per cent do badly, the judges might put it down to the difficult course. Besides, the groom, if he's clever, wouldn't put too much of the mixture in the water-supply but just enough to make the difference. It could be suspicious.'

'You can say that again!' Darcy remarked. 'I reckon it's got a stronger smell than Billingsgate fish-market. I knew there were a lot of dodges connected with horse-racing but I always thought show jumping was a clean business.'

'And so it is!' I sprang to the defence of my sport. 'I know just a bit about it—maybe more than you do, perhaps, Darcy!—and this is the first time anything like this has come my way.'

Jimmy cut short the developing argument with a dash of common sense. 'The point is,' he said 'what are we going to do about this?'

Darcy had an immediate answer. 'We've got to act fast. Today's Monday and the Individual Event is on Wednesday. I don't know how long it takes for drugs to act on horses but this little villain would have to do his stuff, I reckon, not later than tomorrow. He might have done it already! We've no time to lose.'

'What do you propose doing?' I asked.

'I'm thinking aloud now Pat, I haven't worked it out. But the first thing, is for Jimmy and me to see it through. It wouldn't be fair to involve you. After all, you're a

113

competitor and it might look odd if you were to start flinging accusations around. I suppose we ought to report the whole business to the judges and let them sort it out.'

'Frankly, I doubt if that'd work,' I said slowly. 'The judges probably won't meet formally until Wednesday and they'll be scattered all round Rome till then. Even if you did convince most of them that this wasn't a joke, it would take you from now till Wednesday to locate them all. Besides, there'd be a terrible scandal. The word would be certain to leak out and with national prestige so much to the fore, you'd have rows and arguments and riders withdrawing from the Games. Just think what sort of a field-day the Press would have!'

'You're right, Pat,' he said. 'There must be another way.'

Jimmy's eyes were gleaming. 'I think I've got it. There's a party arriving by air tomorrow from Gloucestershire—specially to see the show jumping. Penny Mills is coming and so's our old friend Billy. You remember them, Darcy? —they made up the team we entered for the Prince Philip Cup. Now, if you count in Jane and Jacky, that makes six of us—three pairs.'

'So what?' said Darcy.

'So this. If Pat could wangle us passes for the stables, we could take it in turns to follow this groom-chap wherever he goes. We could work in pairs, one on and two resting, throughout the day and night. He's hardly likely to tip a bucketful of drugs into the water-supply while two of us are breathing down his neck! That way, there'd be no scandal and nobody else would be any the wiser.'

'Sounds all right,' Darcy said grudgingly. I'm not so sure about the night-time, though. In the dark he could give us the slip.'

'Well, at night we could camp out by the water-tank and watch that—once we find out where it is. He'd have to get past us if he wanted to put anything into it,' Jimmy suggested.

'Yes, that's good. It could work.'

'Hey, not so fast,' I butted in. 'This isn't a game you know. This groom isn't just playing hide-and-seek for fun. He's got a lot at stake and he might get desperate if he saw he was being shadowed. You can look after yourself, Darcy, and so can Billy, but I don't want the younger ones, specially the girls, getting involved with criminals. He may use a knife if he gets nasty!'

'Not to worry, Pat,' Darcy said soothingly. 'If we pair up properly—say, Jacky with me, Billy with Jane and Jimmy with Penny—we'd be a match for a little sawn-off chap like him. Besides, he wouldn't risk making too much schemozzle around the place. He won't want to advertise his plans and wake up the rest of the grooms and attendants. You leave it to us, Pat. The main thing is—can you managed to get half a dozen passes for us?'

'I'll try. But you'll have to dress up properly in jodhpurs or breeches and look as though you really are assistant grooms. That goes for you too, Darcy! You must look as though you really care for horses—in both senses of the word.'

'Dash it all,' he said, 'the things I do for England!'

'And for Heaven's sake don't get in the way of the real grooms. Tomorrow is the last day for training and everyone's going to be on edge and rushing round to get ready for the big event. Keep out of their way, won't you?'

'Rely on me, Pat,' Darcy the horse-hater replied. 'I won't get an inch nearer those ungainly quadrupeds than I have to! Well, we'd better be off to round up the others and explain the plot. See you here first thing after breakfast.'

*　　*　　*

That night I kept on wondering whether it had been wise to agree so readily with Jimmy's madcap plan. If it

115

turned out that Darcy had completely misunderstood the overheard conversation in Spanish, then we should all look complete idiots. If, on the other hand, there really was a plot to drug the competing horses, the Three Jays and their friends might be plunged into a dangerous situation and I would never forgive myself for consenting to it. The only thought that brightened my mood was that one problem often drives out another: worrying about the Jays and Company made me quite forget to think about my own hopes and fears for the great day that had almost arrived. I slept soundly that night.

After breakfast next morning, the scarlet Alfa-Romeo slid to a halt at the steps of my hotel and disgorged so many human bodies that even the Roman Passers-by, used as they were to overloaded vehicles, stopped and stared. Jacky emerged from the front seat, where she had been sitting on Penny Mills's lap. Jimmy, Billy and Jane crawled out of the back and Darcy sprawled his long legs on to the pavement from the driver's seat. Several months had gone by since I had seen Penny and I was delighted to notice she was still slim and lithe after her adventures with us in Eire where she lost so much unwanted weight and gained a great horse, Lostboy.* We talked briefly about a couple of point-to-point races he had won since coming over to England. Billy, who had ridden so well in the Prince Philip Cup a couple of years before, was almost a man now. He had grown two or three inches since our last meeting and now I had to raise my head to look him in the eye. We shook hands and chatted about his farm on the other side of Cirencester.

Then the subject turned to more serious and immediate matters. Darcy had briefed the enthusiastic youngsters well and there was little for me to do but warn them against getting over-excited. They were to shadow the South American groom as inconspicuously as they could

* See Three Jays Over the Border.

and, if they did spot him about to drug the water-supply or do anything else suspicious, they were to raise the alarm at once and not try to stop him by themselves. They had arranged to patrol in pairs, as Darcy had suggested, each pair doing two hours on duty and four hours resting. Penny and Jimmy would be first on, then Billy and Jane, and finally Darcy and Jacky. I realized that Darcy had worked it out well so that the worst hours of darkness, the small hours before the dawn would be covered by the stronger pairs, with Billy and himself as the respective leaders. As the night would be warm, they had brought no bedding with them. They hoped to borrow a blanket or two from Paul, my own head groom, and 'kip down', as Darcy put it, alongside the grooms' quarters, when they were not on sentry-go.

*　　*　　*

There is a cricketing story about a county match in which the umpire gave a certain famous batsman out—leg before wicket. The batsman, who had a great reputation for being quick-tempered, stood his ground and shouted down the pitch at the umpire, 'That wasn't out!'

'Oh, yes, it was,' the umpire retorted. 'Wait till you read about it in the papers tomorrow morning!'

On the same basis, Jimmy's and Darcy's plan to foil the drug-plot must have worked—for anyone who read the papers later that week will remember that the show jumping side of the Olympic Games did take place and none of the competing horses behaved very differently from usual. Looking back on the whole affair after an interval, I could not be positive in my inmost heart that the plot ever did exist—but this is the first time I have dared to utter such a disloyal suspicion! Darcy certainly may know some Spanish but it is always possible to get hold of the wrong end of the stick when you overhear

117

a muttered conversation in a foreign language at a nearby table. The Jays and Darcy are, of course, quite positive that their efforts prevented a crime that would have had international repercussions and, as it cannot be proved one way or the other, I feel they ought to keep the credit.

But I am shooting ahead too fast. That Tuesday morning, twenty-four hours before the Individual Jumping Event was due to start, I soon spotted the object of their attention on my way to the practice-area. It would have been quite impossible not to notice the short, swarthy groom because, wherever he went, Penny and Jimmy were dogging his every step. Later that morning, as I was walking the horse back to his box, I saw the groom again. By this time, he looked very jumpy indeed. So would anybody have been in his predicament, for the new patrol of Billy and Jane were breathing down his neck! He was rubbing down a quality chestnut mare that had just finished its morning exercise. Billy and Jane stood either side of him watching every movement. He walked off to fetch another rug from a nearby box and the two 'detectives' followed him, a pace or two to the rear. When he came back, they returned as well and took up their previous positions just behind him. The wretched little man stared at them, then rolled his eyes, shrugged his shoulders in that expressive Latin manner and gazed up at the sky. He must have thought they had escaped from a nearby mental home!

By the middle of the afternoon, when Darcy and Jacky had done their stint and the team of Penny and Jimmy were on their second tour of duty, the groom must have been close to a nervous breakdown. Once or twice he turned on his pursuers and uttered some crackling, expressive sentences. It was lucky that only Darcy out of the six 'trackers' knew any Spanish—and he was off duty at this time. Anyway, I doubt if his command of the language

included epithets of that kind! Penny and Jimmy didn't turn a hair. Like the boy on the burning deck, they stuck doggedly to their task. Finally, the groom retired to his hut. Occasionally, he poked his head round the door and when he saw that Billy and Jane, who had taken over again, were stationed a few paces away, he shot back inside, like a wary hermit crab. He must have lost his nerve entirely, for he didn't venture forth again until next morning—the morning of the Individual Championships, When I arrived at the stables soon after breakfast, a tired but cheerful team of amateur detectives reported that it had been a quiet night, with no alarms or excursions. I thanked them warmly for their efforts and suggested they should fall out, tidy up, have a rest and some food and then take their seats that had been booked months ago in the Olympic Stadium.

And that is the story of how the Three Jays and their friends saved the show jumping side of the Olympic Games from being a fiasco and prevented an international crisis. At least, that still is their firm belief and who am I to deny them their moment of unpublicized glory? One of these days I really must talk to Darcy—in Spanish—and see if he actually does understand the language at all!

CHAPTER SEVEN

OLYMPIC GAMES

THE riders had all gathered at the Piazza di Siena at 6 a.m., the scheduled time for walking the course. The sun was just peeping over the umbrella pines and making a sparkle on the dewy grass. We were not let into the arena until ten past six but meantime we had studied the plan of the course, pinned to the notice board. It was still quite cool and I was glad to have on my wind jacket over my riding-coat. 'Vai,' said an Italian voice and we all surged into the ring on foot. The first three fences were quite straightforward and then a very large water with only a tiny hedge in front of it came as the fourth fence. Very few horses clear this during the competition. Then an unimpressive narrow gate close after the water was followed by brown parallel bars that caught a lot of horses, as it was difficult to see the front pole. Now came the problem fence, a combination of a wall, a triple bar and then parallel bars. The problem was the distance between the last two parts. It was too long for one stride, except perhaps for a flying machine like Sunslave, and too short for two strides still keeping enough impulsion to get over the wide parallel bars.

Riders gathered in anxious groups discussing how to ride this combination. I saw one of the Russians stepping out the distance for a fifth time, hoping that he might have counted wrong the other times.

'Nee ochen kharasho?' I asked him, selecting three of about the ten Russian words I know.

'Nee ochen kharasho,' he confirmed gloomily, meaning —not very good. Forty minutes later one of his compatriots was lying unconscious on the spot where we stood, having had a bad fall which knocked him out.

Indeed we all had good cause for anxiety because this fence spoilt the competition. Many horses fell here including the German Meteor, gold medal winner from Stockholm. Halla, the double gold medallist, was also caught by this. It was not the fault of the Italian course builder, as his original distance, which was quite jumpable, had been changed to this almost unjumpable distance. The rest of the course was big and of Olympic proportions but fair to the horses if they were properly ridden.

The seats of the Piazza di Siena were not filled by the time the first horse was jumping. He had 29¾ faults and the next horse was eliminated. Fifth to go was Raimondo d'Inzeo on Posillipo and with astonishing ease and the admiration of all, he jumped a classical clear round. Only the early birds who arrived before 7.30 a.m. saw this round, and it was to be the only clear of the day.

Sunsalve was the first of the British horses, and David Broome took him round for 16 faults. Halla had 17 faults and then The Rock and Piero d'Inzeo did the second best round for 8 faults.

It soon came round to Flanagan's turn, and I was feeling that it was a bit unkind to ask him to jump a course beyond his physical capabilities. He soon dispelled that fear, taking on the fences like a lion. He did try the impossible at the treble, attempting to jump the third part after only one stride, in spite of my restraining hand. He couldn't believe anyone could put such a silly distance! He very nearly fell, but luckily there was enough room to gather him together before the next fence, a wide parallel bars over water. He finished with 20 faults, a tre-

122

mendous effort for him, and 12 of those faults were for very light touches. I was delighted with him and so was Paul who took him to the horse-box. He was driven back to rest in the cool of the stables as our second round was not until 3.30 in the afternoon.

The next good round was jumped by the grey Argentine horse Final, ridden by Naldo Dasso. He only had one fence down. The French chef d'équipe, Max Fresson, had eight faults on Grand Veneur, to make only the fourth horse with eight faults or less in the first round.

I didn't see Darcy or the Jays at lunchtime as I went to get an hour's rest in the cool of a nearby hotel. When the competition started again in the afternoon, the spectators were grateful for the shade of the trees, a luxury that they did not have the following Sunday while watching the Team competition in the Olympic Stadium. There the sun beat down mercilessly and the only protection provided were paper hats and cardboard eye shields.

Some of the horses that had got a cricket score in the morning were withdrawn in the afternoon, as they had no chance. Many of the horses were jumping in the Team competition on the Sunday, so it was better to save them for that than to risk them again in the Individual competition when they were out of the running for a medal.

The arena was completely hushed when Posillipo came in to do his second round. Raimondo took him carefully round and there was a hiss of pleasure from the crowd as he jumped the water clear, then a hiss of disappointment as he hit the brown poles of the sixth fence. He cleared the treble for the second time but then collected 8 more faults to finish with a total of 12. Only three other horses had a chance of bettering this score.

The next excitement was Sunsalve. There was a gasp from the British when he suddenly stopped at the third fence, an easy wall. David wheeled him back and turned him with determination and really got him going. He

123

jumped bigger and better over each fence until there was only the last to jump. This he hit but his faults had only been 7, to make a total of 23. At the time it seemed likely that at least two other horses would get a lower total than this. Halla had 8, but 17 from the first round put her to 25. The arena was hushed again when Piero came in on The Rock. He went steadily round and collected 8 again to make a total of 16, four faults behind Raimondo.

My excitement came soon afterwards with my second round on Flanagan. He threw his whole heart into the job. He hit the water which I had expected but cleared the brown poles and then we turned for the treble. He jumped it like clockwork and there was a buzz of appreciation from the crowd. The eleventh fence was a wide double of parallel bars and these he just touched while trying to reach for the spread. The next three fences were no problem to him including the last big parallels that had caught Sunsalve each time. A round for 12 and with a little luck it could have been 4! Still a total of 32 wasn't bad, when one looked down the score sheet at totals of $62\frac{1}{2}$, $71\frac{1}{4}$, 65 and 56, and these were from horses whose riders had jumped them a second time because they thought it was worth while.

Final, the Argentine horse, hotted up on his second round and threw away the chance of first gold, then silver and bronze, when he collected 24 faults to put his total to 28. Only two horses were left that could beat Sunsalve's total, but Grand Veneur decided that it was not a medal day for the French by increasing his original 8 faults to $37\frac{1}{4}$ on the second round. Dawn Wofford on Hollandia could do it if she only had the water, but the old horse went to pieces after hitting the treble and his total went up to 44.

That left Raimondo and Piero gold and silver medallists, and David Broome the bronze. A point behind him came George Morris of the U.S.A. and then the Germans,

Winkler and Thiedemann, with 25 and 25¼ faults each.

Flanagan was ninth and, as the Jays said, it was a step in the right direction. In Stockholm he had been tenth in the Individual.

Jimmy said laughingly, 'If you keep moving up one place every four years, you'll be in the running for a medal by the time you're a granny!'

After I had seen Flanagan safely back in the stables and given him a mixture of carrots, boiled sweets and Horlicks tablets, all of which he gobbled up with much relish and a lot of dribble, I went back to the Olympic Village, which I had moved to from my hotel, to have a shower and change. I was feeling a bit tired from our early start, especially as the noise from the Village didn't give one a chance to sleep at night. We got angry about athletes who came in at 1 a.m after they'd finished events at midnight, but they got just as angry with the equestrians who disturbed them when they got up at 4.30 a.m. 'Must you bring your horses down the stairs at that time of the morning?' they would ask us caustically.

'Must you have fencing duels in the bathroom at 1.30 a.m.?' we'd reply.

By the time I had changed I felt much less tired and I phoned Darcy to come and fetch me. We all went out that night to have supper in the Trastevere part of Rome.

We found a restaurant where a cowboy on a grey horse jogged up and down showing the cars where to park. While we at *fettucine*, washed down with some Frascati wine, we were serenaded with Sicilian songs from the musicians. Flanagan and I were both going to have an easy day on Thursday, so there was no hurry. The Jays, Darcy and I relaxed over our dinner and enjoyed the cool of the evening air after the heat of the day.

'It's the participating that counts, you know,' said Darcy suddenly.

'Heavens, d'you think I'm disappointed about today?

125

No, I'm absolutely thrilled that Flanagan went so superbly,' I confirmed to him. 'Wouldn't Baron de Coubertin be proud to hear my words!' I was pulling Darcy's leg as he was referring to the words of the founder of the Modern Olympics.

And what wise words they are, even more true today when so many people look on the Olympic Games as a struggle for international prestige, a kind of unarmed combat but fought just as mercilessly as the real thing. This attitude is so wrong and I tried to speak my thoughts aloud to the Jays, telling them that in any competition, whether it be the Olympic Games or the local Pony Club gymkhana, every competitor must try his hardest but must learn to accept victory with modesty and defeat with a smile. If you win, you must remember that you can't jump big fences without a horse! If you lose, you have nothing to worry about as long as you did your bit and helped the horse to produce his best effort at the right time. I ended by quoting the actual words that Baron de Coubertin used all those years ago: 'The important thing in the Olympic Games is not to win but to take part. The important thing in life is not the triumph but the struggle. The essential thing is not to have conquered but to have fought well.'

There was a long moment's silence and then Jacky broke the spell. 'That's all very well,' she said, 'but what about Darcy's five thousand lire? Think of all the *gelati* we could have eaten on his winnings!'

'If you'd ever caught up with the crooks,' I retorted.

And, as so often happens with the Jays, the episode ended in a roar of laughter, a fitting climax perhaps to their Roman holiday in Olympic Year.

ARMADA BOOKS

BOOKS AVAILABLE INCLUDE:

Mystery and Adventure stories by—
Christine Bernard
Enid Blyton
Dorothy Clewes
John Gunn
Captain W. E. Johns
Ralph Hammond
Malcolm Saville

Pony stories by—
Joanna Cannan
Monica Edwards
Ruby Ferguson
Mary Gervaise
Marguerite Henry
The Pullein-Thompson sisters
Pat Smythe

School stories by—
Elinor M. Brent-Dyer
Anthony Buckeridge
Frank Richards
Noel Streatfeild
Geoffrey Willans & Ronald Searle
P. G. Wodehouse

AND MANY OTHERS, including some Classics.

COMING IN ARMADA

August 1969

PHANTOM HORSE

by
Christine Pullein-Thompson